Secrets of Civil War Spies

Liberty Letters®

Secrets of Civil War Spies

Nancy LeSourd

ZONDERVAN.com/
AUTHORTRACKER
follow your favorite authors

ZONDERkidz™

www.zonderkidz.com

Secrets of Civil War Spies

Previously published as *The Personal Correspondence of Emma Edmonds and Mollie Turner*

Copyright © 2003, 2008 by Nancy Oliver LeSourd

Requests for information should be addressed to:

Zonderkidz, Grand Rapids, Michigan 49530

Library of Congress Cataloging-in-Publication Data

LeSourd, Nancy.-
    Secrets of Civil War spies / Nancy LeSourd.
      p. cm. --(Liberty letters)
    Summary: Letters between two friends, one a student in Richmond, Virginia, and the other a soldier in Washington, D.C., chronicle their experiences during the Civil War, including their work as Union spies and their reliance on God.
      ISBN 978-0-310-71390-6 (softcover : alk. paper)
    1. Spies--Fiction. 2. Nurses--Fiction. 3. Soldiers--Fiction. 4. Christian life--Fiction. 5. United States--History--Civil War, 1861-1865--Fiction. 6. Letters--Fiction.] I. LeSourd, Nancy. Personal correspondence of Emma Edmonds and Mollie Turner. II. Title.
    PZ7.L56268Se 2008
    [Fic]--dc22

                                             2008015007

The story of Emma Edmonds as told by Emma's letters is adapted from *Female Spy*, 1864, republished as *Nurse and Spy in the Union Army*, 1865, by S. Emma E. Edmonds.

Winslow Homer, American, 1836–1910

Young Soldier: Separate Study of a Soldier Giving Water to a Wounded Companion, 1861. Oil, gouache, black crayon on canvas; 260 x 175 mm (14-7/8 x 6-7/8 in.); Cooper-Hewitt, National Design Museum, Smithsonian Institution, Gift of Charles Savage Homer, Jr., 1912-12-110; Photo: Ken Pelka

Zonderkidz is a trademark of Zondervan.

Liberty Letters is a federally registered trademark of Nancy Oliver LeSourd.

Editor: Barbara Scott
Art direction & cover design: Merit Alderink
Interior design: Carlos Eluterio Estrada

Printed in the United States of America

---

08 09 10 11 12 • 5 4 3 2 1

For all the women in America's military, those known and those unknown

Richmond, Virginia

JUNE 17, 1861

Dear Emma,

I couldn't believe my eyes. "Private Franklin Thompson, of the Second Michigan Volunteers," you said. "Requesting donations for the Union Army, ma'am."

While Great Auntie Belle scurried around, loading my arms with linens, food, and medicines, so many questions swirled around in my head. How did you get to Michigan? And what, pray tell, possessed you to enlist in the Union Army? As you carried the supplies outside to the ambulance, I barely heard you whisper, "You'll keep my secret, won't you?"

"Such a nice young man, Mollie," Great Auntie commented, arms filled with more donations.

Young man? This is no man—this is Emma! I thought. *Emma, my good friend.* Last summer I was shocked when you confided in me that you left Canada with your mother's blessing to escape your cruel father. You even fooled everyone in New England, selling books disguised as a boy—one of Mr. Hurlburt's finest door-to-door salesmen. But this? A soldier in the war? Really, Emma! You've gone too far!

Your friend,

Mollie

Washington, D.C.

June 22, 1861

Dear Mollie,

I know I need to explain. When Mr. Hurlburt offered me the chance to work in Flint, Michigan, I jumped at the chance to see more of this adopted country of mine. Mollie, I had to keep up my disguise. After all, I had to make a living.

Then I heard the newsboy cry out, "Fall of Fort Sumter— President's Proclamation—Call for 75,000 men!" It's true I'm not an American. When President Lincoln called for men to fight for my adopted country, I couldn't turn away. I had to help free the slaves. After much prayer, I knew God meant for me to enlist in the Army. So when my friends volunteered for the Second Regiment of the Michigan Volunteer Infantry, I assumed God would make a way for me too. But I missed the height requirement by two inches.

The day my friends left, the people of Flint cheered them on. The boys lined up with their bright bayonets flashing in the morning sunlight. Almost every family had a father, husband, son, or brother in that band of soldiers. The pastor preached a sermon and presented a New Testament to each one. Then as the bands played the "Star-Spangled Banner," the soldiers marched off to Washington. Oh, how I wanted to be with them!

A few weeks later, who should return to Flint, but my old friend from church, William Morse, now *Captain* William Morse who came back to recruit more soldiers for his regiment. This time I was ready. I stuffed my shoes with paper and stood as tall as I could. It worked! I was now Private Franklin Thompson of Company F of the Second Michigan Volunteer Infantry of the United States Army.

When I got to Washington, the army assigned me to be a field nurse. All the field nurses are men, and it doesn't matter if you don't have any training as a nurse. They tell us we'll learn it all from the field surgeons as we go. I reported to the Surgeon in charge and

received my first order to visit the temporary hospitals set up all over the city. Although there are no battle injuries yet, many are sick with typhoid and malaria. There are not enough beds for the sick; not enough doctors to treat them; and not enough medicines and food.

That's why some of us decided to visit the good ladies of Washington and plead with them to donate to the Union. That was the day I saw you again — a most fortunate day for me. I hope you feel the same.

Your friend,

Private Frank Thompson, Company F,
Second Michigan Regiment
(Emma)

Richmond, Virginia

June 28, 1861

Dear Emma,

Of course, I was glad to see you again, but just how do you think you can pull this off—being a private in the United States Army? Sure you can handle nursing duties. But what about shooting and riding a horse, marching and drilling, standing guard and picket duty? Can you keep your secret much longer?

Great Auntie has arranged for our letters to get to each other through her private courier now that the federal government has suspended mail to the Southern states. She is delighted I want to write to a Federal soldier. I'll address your letters to Frank so there is no suspicion. Is it all right to call you Emma in the letter? I don't want to give you away.

Great Auntie makes no secret of her support of the North, as you saw from her willingness to part with supplies for the Union. To the great embarrassment of my Richmond kin, Great Uncle Chester is now a surgeon with the Union Army and Great Auntie Belle is an outspoken supporter of President Lincoln. If Daddy were still alive, I'm sure he would agree. At least that's what I think. Momma seems to think differently.

When Momma and I arrived at Mrs. Whitfield's home today to sew uniforms for the soldiers, we heard angry voices before we even entered the room. Mrs. Whitfield told the ladies she had personally delivered a handwritten invitation to Miss Elizabeth Van Lew and her mother to join us to sew for the Confederate soldiers, but the Van Lews refused to come.

"Let's not forget they sent their daughter, Betty, to that Quaker school in Philadelphia," an outraged Mrs. Morris reminded everyone. "They filled that child's head with abolition talk, and it changed her forever."

"That they did," Mrs. Forrest agreed. "And when Mr. Van Lew died, Betty talked her mother into freeing all their slaves."

Aunt Lydia added, "I heard they even sent one of their slave girls up north to Philadelphia for her schooling and paid for it all!"

I watched the ladies ram their needles through the flannel shirts they were stitching with as much force as the words they were speaking. Personally, I think these ladies are petty gossips. So what if Miss Van Lew believes what the Union does? Is that a crime? It seems so. If they only knew what I believed, they would not permit me in their company. A Southern girl with Northern thoughts. I kept my head down as these ladies spoke. I didn't want them to see the fire in my eyes.

I excused myself as soon as I could and slipped out without much notice. No one pays much attention to a sixteen-year-old girl these days. The women worry about their boys and men and speak endlessly of the impending battles. Their attention is not on the comings and goings of someone like me.

I took this package to the place the courier designated to drop off our letters. I may have knitted for the Confederates today, but this pair of socks is included for you, my adventurous Union friend. Perhaps they will keep your feet from blistering on those long marches.

Your friend,

Mollie

Washington, D.C.

July 1, 1861

Dear Mollie,

Thanks for thinking about how to protect my secret. To tell the truth, I like reading my name again. To these men, I am just Frank, but to you, my good friend, I am Emma. I keep your letters tucked inside my shirt so no one can read them. I suppose for now, though, you should continue to address your letters to Frank, but just call me E in the letter. If I should lose a letter, I don't want to risk being found out.

As for riding a horse or shooting a gun, what do you think I did all those years when I was growing up on our farm in New Brunswick, Canada? I can outride and outshoot most anyone—thank you, Miss Mollie. If God has called me to this, then he has prepared me and equipped me to do what I must do. Farming was no harder work. Just try chopping and clearing the land some time, Mollie. Why, you should have seen me swing my ax to hew beams from timber as fast as the next boy. No sirree, if I'm found out, it will not be because I failed to hold my own with these brave men.

Washington is overrun with soldiers. White tents dot the landscape all around the city. The Capitol and the White House shelter hundreds of soldiers, who sit around playing cards and wait for action. Thousands of soldiers drill in the streets. Blasts from bugles and the rat-tat-tat of drums fill the air. All are eager to fight. The rebellion should be put down quickly.

Your friend,

Emma

Richmond, Virginia

JULY 4, 1861

Dear Emma,

Richmond celebrated Independence Day today, but I had to wonder, is it independence from England years ago or independence from the North it celebrates? Sissy asked me to go with her today to the camps outside the city to watch the soldiers drill. She may be two years older than I, but she has such romantic notions about this war. She thinks she can send her Lemuel off to war and he will return to her a hero. Our friends ride out to the camps every day. They dress up, bring their picnic foods, and wait for the drills to end so they can socialize with the soldiers. It all seems so silly to me—this partying with soldiers. Soldiers and girls alike think we will simply wallop the North in one big battle, and then it'll all be over. I'm not so sure.

I don't agree with you that this will be a short war. You think the boys in blue will crush the boys in gray. But here in Richmond, we too have white tents dotting the landscape like snow. Our soldiers march day and night, eager to meet the enemy. We too have hundreds, if not thousands, of young men who are certain we will capture Washington and take over the White House and Capitol where your soldiers now lounge. I do not think victory will come so easily, my dear friend, not to either side.

As the South Carolina regiment marched past us, the girls waved their handkerchiefs and cheered. They debated which regiment is the most handsome. The general consensus of our friends is that the boys from South Carolina are definitely the best looking, although the Texas regiment is a close runner-up with their rugged good looks. You see how deep their thoughts go about this war, Emma. Skin deep.

My attention was on two women handing out food and flowers to the South Carolinians. A murmur spread through the crowd. It was Miss Van Lew and her mother who smiled as they handed out their gifts. Miss Van Lew called out, "May God grant victory to

the righteous!" Very clever. She didn't say which side is righteous! But the boys seemed to enjoy her attentions just the same. The women who whispered behind their fans as they watched certainly were wondering why a supposed Yankee loyalist brings food to the Confederate soldiers!

Great Auntie wrote that I can't return to Mrs. Pegram's school next fall. For the past two years since Daddy died, the Greats (that's what I call them) have paid for my education. Mrs. Pegram, with three sons fighting for the South, returned their money, and told them that Federal dollars are worthless to purchase an education for a Confederate girl. She said they could exchange their money for Confederate scrip and resend the funds for my semester's tuition.

Of course, that made the Greats furious. As much as they value my education, they won't put it ahead of their beliefs. Great Auntie prepared a box of books from Great Uncle Chester's library and sent them to me to study on my own. It's not the same though. This war is turning everything upside down.

My good friend Charlie brought the newspapers tonight and tried to cheer me up. The Confederates captured the Union steamer, the *St. Nicholas*. The paper reported that Madame LaForce—an outrageously dressed, veiled lady—boarded at Baltimore with great fanfare and seven dress trunks. Madame LaForce flirted with the sailors in French and English, but you should have seen her later when she pulled pistols and swords, not dresses, out of those trunks. Madame LaForce was really Colonel Thomas! "She" created such a distraction that no one noticed the eight men who boarded the *St. Nicholas* at Port Comfort that day and then joined Colonel Thomas in the attack on the ship that night. Later, the *St. Nicholas* captured several other Union ships filled with supplies that can now go to the Confederate Army.

My good friend Emma posing as a Union soldier, and a Confederate colonel posing as a lady. All is definitely not what it first appears!

Your friend,

Mollie

Richmond, Virginia

July 7, 1861

Dear E,

I just got your most recent letter and will do as you suggest. I want to do all I can to help you keep this secret.

Yesterday Sissy married Lemuel Hastings. And today he enlisted in the Army of the Confederate States of America. Sissy is determined to follow him wherever he is sent to fight. Momma told Sissy that her place is in Richmond with the ladies, sewing uniforms, knitting socks, and rolling bandages. Sissy bounced out of the room with her skirts swishing behind her as she tossed her head full of blonde curls. "I shall follow Lemuel to the ends of the earth," she called back to us over her shoulder. "It is my wifely duty."

Sissy has always been impulsive, but she gave Momma only three days to pull together a wedding. Even with the help of Momma's kin and their servants, there was hardly enough time to decorate the parlor, bake and display the cakes and sweets, and deliver all the invitations. Sissy decided there should be no wedding gifts. Not that anyone has any money to spare right now, anyway. In her usual fashion, she turned that all to her advantage. In her noblest of voices, she announced to one and all that they should each bring a necessity for the Confederate soldiers and deposit it in the box by the front door.

I honestly don't believe that Sissy understands what this is all about. Ever since Daddy died, it's like Sissy refuses to grow up. She'd rather pretend nothing is wrong than face facts. That's how she is with Lem and this war. She probably thinks she will pull on her white kidskin gloves, button up her dainty shoes, and swirl her hooped skirt around her as she travels by train or coach to the nearest town where Lemuel's unit is stationed. Then when he is off duty, they will dance the night away at the local town hall.

Your friend,

Mollie

Richmond, Virginia

July 10, 1861

Dear E,

Sissy and I walked to Pizzini's for ice cream. With each bite, Sissy complained about the Union blockade of our ports. If it succeeds, we will be unable to get the necessities of life. To Sissy, this means her tea and sweets. She hoards sugar in a tin can in her room. She says she may have to suffer many things in this war, but she will not suffer the loss of her sugar.

Sissy says she wants this silly war to get started so those horrible Yanks can be put in their place and her dear Lem can come home to her. I suppose that's what you are to most of those I know here: a horrible Yank.

The Northern papers Great Auntie sent me urge you Federals to stop the "Rebel Congress" from meeting here next week. "Forward to Richmond! On to Richmond! The Rebel Congress shall not meet." I admit I'm frightened. Momma too. She speaks in hushed tones with the Richmond kin. They are especially quiet around Sissy. They don't want her to be frightened for Lemuel. But how can she not be frightened? Won't he be one of the ones defending our dear city?

Will you be the one attacking it? I do not like this at all.

Your friend,

Mollie

Richmond, Virginia

JULY 17, 1861

Dear E,

Just three days until the Confederate government meets here. People talk quietly, especially when there are children in the room. It's not like they don't notice. The adults pretend we're safe in our homes, but you can hear the sounds of the guns and drummers on the battlefields not that far away. Sissy sits at the window, twisting her handkerchief first one way then the other. Momma told her to knit to keep her fingers busy. Sissy tried, but gave up in frustration, dropping more stitches than she could keep on the needles.

I suggested a walk. Old men spoke in hushed tones in doorways. Women whispered to one another behind fans. Only the youngest children seemed carefree. Would the Union win and be "On to Richmond"? What about the dozens of fathers, husbands, brothers, and sons that enlisted? Would they return?

Tonight Momma and the Richmond ladies gathered at Aunt Lydia's home to roll bandages and pick lint for packing wounds. Momma asked Sissy and me to come with her. I wish we were knitting socks and sewing uniform shirts. I don't like preparing for wounds and cuts and bloody bodies. I shudder to think of it. Sissy tries to join in, but I can see on her face she is wondering if the bandage she rolls tonight will be on her husband tomorrow.

Your friend,

Mollie

Centerville, Virginia

JULY 19, 1861

Dear Mollie,

When we began our march to Manassas, the bands played patriotic songs, and the soldiers cried out enthusiastically, "On to Richmond!" But as I rode in the ambulance, watching those long lines of bayonets gleaming and flashing in the sunlight, I thought that many—very many—of these men might never return.

The first night of the march, we stayed in Fairfax. The men were exhausted from the long march in the July heat. I felt a bit guilty as I had ridden almost the entire way. Early the next morning, the drummers and buglers sounded reveille, and the whole camp was up and marching again. This time I was with them.

James Vincent, one of the soldiers I met when I enlisted, marched alongside me for most of the morning. He is tall with dark wavy hair and abundant energy. Sometimes I had to march double step to keep up with him. When I asked him what he thought about the sacrifice of so many lives that is sure to occur, he said he'd willingly give his life that the slave might become free. "There are probably as many reasons to fight for the North as there are soldiers in blue," James said, "but there is no greater reason than the emancipation of enslaved men. I know the heart of God and it cannot condone that any child of God should be the property of another man. They call this the rebellion, but it is man's rebellion against God that causes him to want to control another human being. That is the real rebellion that we must fight against."

It was so hot that I felt faint. Thankfully James marched with me. The more we talked, the more it kept my mind off the awful heat. There was little water. We didn't even cross a stream where we could fill our canteens. I kept licking my lips to moisten them, but that only made it worse. About noon, we heard sharp volleys of

muskets, and I jumped at the sound. It turned out to be our advance guard firing at anything that moved. Every hour, we expected to meet the enemy. Just about the time my racing heart would calm down, we'd hear another volley and it would be pounding again. I have no idea what to expect once the battle begins. I just hope I am up to the task.

The army moved steadily on and investigated every field, building, and ravine for miles in front and to the right and to the left. When we reached Centerville, we stopped for the night. Tired from two days of marching, the men fell in a heap. Many of their feet were blistered raw. We took linen, bandages, lint, and ointment and ministered to their blistered trodden feet. My feet held up well thanks to your well-knitted socks, Mollie. Thank you. And I was never so thankful for a canteen full of water.

The surgeons ordered the field nurses to prepare for the coming battle by securing several buildings, including a stone church, as makeshift hospitals and operating theaters. I helped set up medicine bottles, bandages, and the surgeon's tools. I dropped one of the glass vials and it shattered all over the floor. I apologized over and over again to the field nurse with me. He told me not to worry, and helped me sweep up the shards of glass. We didn't speak again, but I could tell he was just as anxious as I was, even though he had steadier hands. I've never been in combat before. I don't know what I would do if I had to assist a surgeon while he amputated an arm or leg of one of my new friends, like James. I've got to figure out a way to focus my mind and not focus on *la mort subité*. So sorry, Mollie, I slipped back into French Canadian words. I can't focus on sudden death, but must remember that God, the giver of life, is always with me.

Late in the evening, our chaplain and his wife and I walked through the camp to see how the boys were doing, on this, the eve of their first battle. Some wrote letters home and enclosed keepsakes like locks of hair or rings, just in case. Others read their Bibles. Others sat in groups, talking in low tones. Many stretched out on the ground, wrapped up in their blankets, oblivious to the dangers of the coming day.

We were about to return to our quarters when we heard singing coming from a little grove of trees not far from camp. As we came closer, we could hear the words of the hymn sung with great feeling:

> *O, for a faith that will not shrink, though pressed by every foe;*
> *That will not tremble on the brink of any earthly woe.*
> *That will not murmur or complain beneath the chastening rod*
> *But in the hour of grief and pain will lean upon its God.*

A fellow soldier, Willie Lyman, led the prayer meeting and prayed for loved ones at home, for his comrades, and for victory in battle. And with great emotion, he pled with God to comfort and support his mother if he should die. Others joined him in prayer, and then one by one, they shared their faith in the power of the gospel of Christ. My new friend, James, was there too. He was steady and calm on this night before battle. He stood up and read from the Bible—the 23rd Psalm. His booming voice pierced the dark, night sky as he read, "Yea, though I walk through the valley of the shadow of death, I will fear no evil, for thou art with me."

I could not help wondering if the Confederates on the other side of Bull Run were also grouped together praying for victory. *Oh, Lord, help us all.*

Your friend,

E

Richmond, Virginia

JULY 19, 1861

Dear E,

We awoke to the news that General Beauregard won the first fight with the Union at Blackburn's Ford near Manassas. The city today bustled with excitement and anxiety—excitement because the Confederates scored a victory and anxiety because we wondered at what cost.

Surgeons in ambulances, our bandages with them, raced to Manassas. Sissy was desperate to go too, but Momma would not permit it. Word came that more fighting is expected and that the skirmish yesterday was just a prelude. Sissy has given up twisting her handkerchief and twists her hair now. "I just have to know if Lem is all right," she said to me more than once today.

I have to know if you're all right. Were you there? Did you fight today? Are you well?

I caught Sissy packing tonight. I told Momma because I knew Sissy would do something crazy—like leave in the middle of the night—just to make sure Lemuel is safe. But *she* would not be safe. Sissy was angry with me, but I don't care. I love my sister.

✷ ✷

Two days later—July 21:

I tried to get back into Sissy's good graces by walking with her after church at St. Paul's to the Spotswood Hotel for news. The First Lady moved quietly about the lobby, speaking first to one and then to another mother, wife, or daughter of our men and boys in gray who were fighting that day.

We overheard someone tell her that the fighting has been going on since six o'clock this morning at Manassas. Sissy swallowed hard and clenched her hands. I gave her my handkerchief so she would have something to twist.

It was all I could do to get Sissy to leave the Spotswood Hotel tonight to return home. She was sure the first news would come swiftly to the hotel because the wives of so many colonels and generals as well as the First Lady of the Confederacy were there. True enough. I could see in their eyes that they would stay up all night until they had news.

It is the waiting, the uncertainty that is so difficult to bear.

Your friend,

Mollie

Washington, D.C.

JULY 23, 1861

Dear Mollie,

I'm safe, but how I got back here is another story! The battle began very early with column after column of soldiers marching over green hills and through the hazy valley in the remains of the moonlight. We heard no drums or bugles — only muffled marching of soldiers and the rumble of cannons. The three divisions each took a position along Bull Run Creek. As morning light broke, the two armies were in plain sight of each other. I delivered my horse to Jack, our hospital man, with strict orders to remain where he was. I might need my horse at any moment.

Chaplain B, Mrs. B, and I stood there, waiting for the first casualty. I had no idea what to do if they brought me wounded to tend! They'd know right away that I was no nurse. I stared at Mrs. B. Her narrow-brimmed leghorn hat sat firmly on her dark brown hair and framed her pale face and blue eyes. She had her silver-mounted, seven-shooter pistol tucked in her belt, a canteen of water swung over one shoulder, a flask of brandy over the other shoulder, and a haversack with lint, ointment, adhesive plaster, and bandages hanging by her side. Mrs. B said she had seen many battles traveling with her husband. She's learned from the field nurses what to do, and soldier or not, no one was going to turn her away on a day like this. She looked so confident, and I felt so unprepared and scared. I thought, *Well, I'll just watch what she does and do it too.*

As the battle commenced, I raced to one of our wounded. When I raised his head, now covered in blood, I saw it was Willie Lyman. *No! Not Willie!* Another nurse and I carried him on a stretcher to the ambulance. I told Willie not to give up, but his breathing was so shallow. God, why Willie? He's much, much too young.

I spent most of the early morning and on into the day going from one fallen soldier to another to tend their wounds. I was numb.

I kept going through the motions of tipping water from my canteen into blood-caked mouths and packing wounds with lint, but my mind kept going back to Willie. Would he survive?

At the request of the surgeon, I rode back to Centerville for a fresh supply of lint and bandages. When I returned, the field was covered with our wounded, dead, and dying. I searched for Willie but didn't find him. Mrs. B galloped toward me with all possible speed. About fifty canteens hung from the pommel of her saddle. "The troops are famished for water!" she exclaimed.

I mounted my horse, and we raced to the nearest spring where we filled the canteens as quickly as we could. Minnie balls fell thick and fast around us but we dodged those bullets. My hands shook so hard I lost as much water out of the canteen as I was trying to scoop in from the spring. The only thing that kept me going was thinking of Willie. If he could face the danger, then so could I. At least that's what I told myself, but my heart was pounding as loud as the horses' hoofbeats.

When Chaplain B's horse was shot dead right out from under him, I screamed. Chaplain B shouted, "I'm okay." It took a full hour before my heart stopped racing. For the next three hours, we went back and forth to the spring, filling canteens and distributing the water among the wounded. Then the Confederates pushed us back and captured the spring. Our source of water was gone. I was terrified. How were we going to get more water? How would we help the wounded soldiers once these canteens ran out?

I worked among the wounded alongside the surgeons and other nurses in the field, doing whatever they told me to do. I could not think about Willie or any of these poor men. I had to focus on the task at hand. Cool water. Fresh lint. On to the next soldier. More water. Another bandage. We were nearly out of water, when Colonel Cameron rode up and dashed along the line shouting, "Come on, boys, the Rebels are in full retreat." But they were not. In fact, fresh support troops had arrived to help them. The enemy advanced, and the panic-stricken crowds who had come to watch the fighting now joined the Federal troops retreating towards Washington.

On orders, I returned to the stone church in Centerville as fast as my horse would take me and began helping the wounded. Many would not survive the horrible surgeries where shattered arms and legs are amputated. I wasn't prepared for the vast numbers of these surgeries happening so fast in this tiny church. I felt sick at the horrible screams of agony. I tried to be a good soldier and field nurse, but I couldn't take it. I fought against waves of nausea. The surgeon in charge must have noticed because he sent me outside to tend to those waiting for their surgeries. I was never so thankful for fresh air and to be out of the stench of that blood-soaked makeshift hospital. As I packed fresh lint into their wounds, I tried not to think of what was to come for these poor men.

We were so busy taking care of wounded or dying soldiers out in the field that we didn't notice the Federal troops had pulled back and left us in Rebel-controlled territory. One of the wounded said he had seen the Federals retreating. But surely they wouldn't leave the hospital of their own wounded in the clutches of the enemy!

I rushed to the heights and gasped. The soldier was right. No Federals anywhere. Everything in me wanted to hightail it out of there and get back to Washington before the Rebels gained control over Centerville. But what about the wounded men? And the surgeons? I had to make my way back to the stone church to warn them, even if it meant I was captured.

I reported what I had seen to the surgeon in charge. He signaled to the other field surgeons that they were to finish up quickly, gather their surgical tools, and get back to Washington. I gave water to as many of the wounded as I could from my canteen. The soldiers begged me to leave before the Rebels arrived. They said the Rebels would not let me tend their wounds or give them water to drink. I knew they were right, but to leave them seemed so cowardly. If I stayed, what good could I do for the wounded from the inside of a Rebel prison? I left water as near their reach as possible before I left.

That night was exceedingly dark and the rain came down in torrents. I climbed a fence, crossed some lots, and made my

way to Washington as quickly as possible. I had neither food nor water, but I kept safe the special items those wounded soldiers had entrusted into my care—letters, rings, pictures of loved ones, and messages that I would later send to their families. All the way back, I couldn't help but think about this Sabbath day. While church members—Northern and Southern—fell to their knees in prayer and church bells rang out the call to worship, their brothers, fathers, and sons fell to their knees struck with bullets as bugles and drums beat out the call to arms.

Chaplain and Mrs. B were thrilled to see me. Thinking I was already a prisoner, they had taken my horse with them. I was thrilled to see my horse had not fallen into enemy hands and would be there to ride with me another day. I asked about the men who had fallen that day. When Mrs. B told me Willie Lyman, though gravely wounded, had not died, I fell to my knees. He had been my inspiration to make it through this day, and I was so thankful. The ambulance took him to a hospital in Washington. Tentatively, I asked about my new friend, James. Chaplain B said James would live to fight another day

It was a terrible, terrible battle for the Federals. If the Rebels had only kept coming, they might have captured Washington. I don't know why they didn't, but I am glad.

Your friend,

E

Richmond, Virginia

July 23, 1861

Dear E,

Yesterday, we were up before dawn. I don't think Sissy, Momma, or I slept much last night. Word of the battle and victory for the South spread quickly. Richmond should have been excited, but the women just wanted to know one thing—the fate of our loved ones.

Sissy and I stayed at the Virginia Central train station hoping for word of Lemuel. We waited for the train from Manassas in the pouring rain until after ten at night. When it was clear we would get no word, we went home, tired and soaked to the skin. Sissy fell asleep as soon as I helped her out of her wet clothes.

Early this morning we went back down to the train depot. President Davis arrived from Manassas on the first train and told the crowd that the Confederates sent the Yankees running toward Washington. The papers all declared victory, but we cannot celebrate until we know Lemuel is safe. Dozens of soldiers, bloody and wounded, poured out of the train cars. Men and boys with wounded arms and legs on stretchers. Bloody bandages on the heads and arms of those who could walk. Men and boys limping and on crutches. Where were our lively marchers now? No drums or bugles welcomed these soldiers. Only women and girls, anxious to see someone they dearly love. Sissy stood on a box and looked at each face for her Lem.

This afternoon, the train brought another load of desperate soldiers from Manassas. We saw Elijah Wilson, our good friend who had enlisted with Lem. Sissy raced to Elijah, whose head was bloody and bandaged. His family's farm was too far away so we brought him home with us for the night.

Elijah's wound is not too deep, and he should be fine. He enjoyed the good food Momma prepared, and we got much news from him about the battle. Elijah did not know Lem's present whereabouts, but he had seen him toward the end of the battle. At that time, he'd still been standing strong. That news comforted Sissy, and she brightened enough to share her sugar with Elijah in his tea.

When Elijah spoke of the falling Federals, though, I couldn't help but think of you. I hope you weren't one of those in blue who fell on Sunday, the Sabbath day of our Lord.

Tonight my friend Charlie brought me a copy of the *Examiner*. The paper said, "By the work of Sunday we have broken the backbone of the invasion and utterly broken the spirit of the North." Perhaps so. But trains continue to bring in the dead and the wounded, and homes have turned into hospitals.

Charlie told us that hundreds of Union prisoners were arriving at the train station and being marched through the streets to Liggon's tobacco factory on Main Street. He said there were more than a thousand prisoners there. If there are Federals here now in our city, then there must be Confederates captured as well. This has Sissy severely agitated as she wonders if Lem is one of them. She twists both hair and handkerchief. Momma had her knead some bread tonight just to keep her hands as well as her mind busy.

Your friend,

Mollie

Washington, D.C.

JULY 25, 1861

Dear Mollie,

Just a quick note to let you know I am fine. The nurses are sleeping in shifts now and making rounds of the hospitals here. So far, due to my inexperience, I have not attended any more surgeries. I steel myself to pack the wounds with fresh lint. I'm getting better now. Not quite so much nausea.

I've determined to keep these men in the best spirits possible. I tell them stories of my farm days growing up in New Brunswick. Their favorite one is how we moved a house in winter on runners pulled by oxen through the snow. They say that is why I am so strong for someone so small. I tell them, "Give me an ax, and I'll best all of you in felling timber." So far no one has taken me up on the challenge.

So far, so good. What I wouldn't give to see their faces if I told them the truth!

Your friend,

E

Richmond, Virginia

JULY 26, 1861

Dear E,

Oh glory hallelujah! After days of waiting and searching among the wounded, Sissy finally heard from Lem. He is safe. Determined more than ever to follow him, Sissy packed her bags and wouldn't listen at all to Momma, who begged her to stay. We took Sissy to the train depot this morning, and now it's Momma who twists her handkerchief. I kissed Sissy good-bye and told her I'd go with her the next time. That only agitated Momma more. Sissy talked a blue streak because she's so excited about seeing Lem again. Lem was promoted to captain for his bravery in action at the Battle of Manassas, and Sissy stayed up all night to stitch him a new shirt to show him how proud she is of him. I must admit; it's a huge improvement over her first effort — the shirt with two right sleeves.

After we saw Sissy off, Momma and I went to Aunt Lydia's to pick some more lint and roll some more bandages. But mostly, it was to get the news. And we were not disappointed! Did you know that women traveled from Washington to the battle in their buggies and coaches with their picnic hampers, brandy, and fruit? Well, they got the surprise of their lives when they had to step over dead soldiers to scurry back to the safety of their Washington homes. My Richmond kin told Momma they always knew Northern women lacked compassion. "Not at all like our own Sally Tompkins," the ladies murmured.

Judge Robertson moved his family to the country and turned over his house at Main and Third streets to Miss Sally to use as a hospital. She stocked it with extra beds, clean linens, medicines, and nourishing foods. The ladies approve of her decision to use her family fortune to relieve our men's suffering. They all plan to help Miss Sally in any way they can.

As quick as they were to praise Sally Tompkins, they tripped

over each other to condemn another of our Richmond ladies, Miss Betty Van Lew. "Always peculiar in her thinking," they said. "A Northerner through and through," they agreed. "Dangerous to the Confederacy," they feared.

Mrs. Adams exclaimed, "I heard the Yankees had not even had time to peruse their new surroundings before Miss Van Lew was at the prison door begging to nurse them." Mrs. Whitfield added, "Of course that young prison warden, Lieutenant Todd, put her in her place and told her under no uncertain terms would a Southern lady do such a thing."

"But you know what she did then?" exclaimed Mrs. Adams. "She went from office to office until she could convince someone to let her visit the Federal prisoners!"

Mrs. Martin added, "I heard she brings them sweets and books and stationery."

Mrs. Logan put down her lint basket and leaned across the table. She whispered, "You know, dear ladies, it is not so much what she takes in which concerns me ..." They all leaned forward eagerly. "It's what she brings out!"

This afternoon the man who delivers our letters and packages asked me if I was a girl who loved to learn. When I acted surprised, he said my great aunt, on more than one occasion, had mentioned that a package contained books. He said another of his customers in Richmond has a very fine library and he might be able to persuade her to lend me some books. I was so surprised, I forgot to ask her name.

E, I have to ask. I have wondered how you are able to take care of, well you know, your bodily needs. How in the world, when you "tend to business," do you keep your secret?

Your friend,

Mollie

Richmond, Virginia

JULY 27, 1861

Dear E,

Today was the second day Momma and I volunteered our services to Miss Sally Tompkins at the Robertson Hospital. Miss Sally is well suited for the task. There are twenty-two beds in the hospital, and although Miss Sally is not in the army, it's clear who the general is here!

I think even the Greats would be impressed with Miss Sally—despite her strong Confederate leanings. Especially, Great Uncle Chester. As you know, he loves it when Southern women take matters into their own hands. I've heard him say more than once that Southern women are the ones who need to rebel!

The Robertson Hospital is spotless. I think Miss Sally takes the motto, "Cleanliness is next to godliness" quite seriously. She insists that the floors, bed linens, clothes, and the surgeon's tools are scrubbed clean. I haven't cleaned this much in all my life. Her house servants are there to help her, but she is a bundle of energy herself. She carries her medicine kit on her belt at all times and ministers to the needs of these fallen soldiers.

As much as she cares for the body, she cares for the soul as well. She holds a prayer meeting and a Bible study every night. Momma and I stayed for tonight's meeting, and it brought tears to my eyes. Her love for the Lord is deep and strong. If a soldier is too ill or wounded to make it to the room for Bible study and prayer, she goes to his bedside to pray with him.

I finally have a pass to visit Great Auntie next month so I can see your secret life. Speaking of secrets, did you hear about the arrest of Mrs. Greenhow in Washington for spying! She is under house arrest with her young daughter. The Richmond ladies, some of whom knew her well from Washington when their husbands were senators and congressmen, cannot believe it. Momma says that wars are times for secrets and intrigue. Momma's right.

This time when the man who delivers our packages from Great Auntie stopped by, he had an extra slip of paper. This was what was written on it:

Miss Elizabeth Van Lew

2311 Grace Street on Church Hill

He nodded at me and said, "Her library is superb. She's expecting you. Perhaps you'd like to borrow some of her books." Then he turned on his heels and left without another word.

Your friend,

Mollie

Washington, D.C.

JULY 29, 1861

Dear Mollie,

Willie Lyman, the boy I wrote to you about who led the prayer meeting the night before the battle, died early this morning. His wounds were too grave for him to recover. After Chaplain B prayed with him, Willie asked me to write to his mother. I took down every word he said, but it was all I could do to keep the tears from flowing on the paper and smearing the ink. His last words were, "Tell Mother I died trusting in Jesus." I trembled as I cut a lock of his hair to put in the envelope with the letter. Oh, if only his dear mother could have been here to hold his hand. His soul winged its way to heaven as the first rays of the early morning light shown down.

I know there will be deaths, but this soldier was so good, and so young. My heart was very heavy as I left the hospital ward. I walked around the city for hours to try to clear my mind. James said that there is no greater sacrifice than to lay down one's life for another. I thought of the sacrifice of Willie's life—the wife Willie would never have, the children who would not call him Daddy, and the lives he could have touched if he had not died so young.

I returned to camp and found James to tell him of Willie's death. He took off his cap and bowed his head. After a few moments, he said, "God was with Willie Lyman just like he prayed the night before battle—nothing can separate us from the love of God, not even death, Frank."

Your friend,

F

Richmond, VA

July 29, 1861

Dear E,

President Davis requested that we honor Sunday as a day of thanksgiving for the Confederate victory. While the preacher spoke about the hand of God being with the South, I had to wonder if the hand of God was with the North. Is God with you only when you win a battle — or is he there when you lose as well?

Momma misses Sissy. She thinks Sissy is too young to travel alone, especially in wartime, but Sissy is a married woman now and eighteen. She'll be fine. Momma busied herself on the Sabbath making a pie, using some of Sissy's precious hoarded sugar. Momma never would have done that if she weren't so worried.

Charlie came by with the *Examiner.* He's itching to go to war, but at fourteen, his parents forbid him to enlist until he turns sixteen. They say a boy must be at least eighteen before he can enlist, but I know boys sixteen and seventeen who wear the gray jackets of the Confederacy. I suppose if you fooled the recruiters, they could too. Charlie practices drumming the signals. He wants to join his brother's unit as a drummer boy.

Charlie drank lemonade on the veranda made from one of Momma's last lemons (without Sissy's sugar). The paper praised all the true women of Richmond who've been giving their aid to the wounded. But when it told of the kindnesses Miss Betty and her mother have shown toward the Yankee prisoners just four blocks from their home, it practically charged them with treason. "The course of these two females in providing them with delicacies, buying them books, stationery, and papers, cannot but be regarded as an evidence of sympathy amounting to an endorsement of the cause and conduct of these Northern vandals."

Wait until the Richmond ladies read this! Miss Van Lew will never be invited to sew with these ladies again. Somehow, I don't

think she will mind at all. When Charlie left, I went for a walk. A half hour later I found myself at the top of Church Street in front of the Van Lew mansion set high on one of Richmond's most lovely hills overlooking the city.

Miss Van Lew opened the door. No servants or slaves at this house. "Yes?" she asked. I stood there staring at her. She was just as Momma and her kin had described—a small woman with blonde hair and a sharp angular nose. Momma's kin called her "a little bird" and, standing there staring at her, I had to agree. This tiny woman could not possibly be a danger to the Confederate cause.

"I'm Mollie Turner," I said as if that should explain it all.

"What can I do for you, Miss Turner?" she replied.

A wonderful aroma poured out of the house. As this was a fast day for the Confederacy, I was surprised by the smells of rich food coming from Miss Van Lew's home. I was already weak from fasting, and these reminders of good home cooking didn't help at all.

"Don't you know why I am here?" I asked. She just stood there stone-faced. This wasn't going well at all. I was sure the courier who delivered Great Auntie's packages to me and who delivered mail to Miss Van Lew had spoken to her of me. Why else would he have given me her name and address? Miss Van Lew studied me for a few moments and then invited me in.

I stepped inside before she changed her mind. I walked down the hall and noticed her dining room table set for a celebration. The silver was gleaming and the smells coming from the kitchen were definitely that of a turkey roasting.

"It's a fast day," I said simply.

"Indeed it is," she replied, "a prayer and fasting day for the success of the Confederacy."

"You're not fasting,"

"No, indeed I am not," she replied.

"Why?"

"I choose not to," she said.

"You're not only *not* fasting; you're having a feast," I said accusingly.

"Hmmm" was all she said in response. She met my gaze coolly, and then continued, "Miss Turner, what do you think about this Great War? Which side of the war has the most compelling reasons for winning?"

"I'm a Virginian!" I replied as if that answered it all.

"I am too!" she replied with a smile.

"Virginians must stick with each other … and with the Southern states."

"Must we?" she asked.

"Why, of course. It's the right thing to do."

"Why is it right?"

I couldn't answer her. The truth is I don't think it is right. I think Virginians can have more than one opinion about this war.

"I heard you nurse at Robertson Hospital."

What else does she know about me?

"I heard you visit at Libby Prison," I countered.

"There is much one can learn while talking to soldiers," she said. "Whether imprisoned or in the hospital. You should keep your eyes and ears open, Mollie, you may learn something useful."

I couldn't believe what I was hearing. Was she suggesting I spy on the soldiers — our Southern wounded men — right there in Miss Sally's hospital?

"Now, you came for books, didn't you?" Still startled, I said nothing and followed her as she turned on her heels smartly and clicked down the long hall to her library. Inside was the largest room I had ever seen filled with books, hundreds of them. "Eager to learn, I hope. Choose what you will."

I couldn't move. My mind was racing. She studied me intently. Finally, she selected a book and handed it to me. I said a quick thank you and bolted down the hall and out the door. I raced down the steps as fast as I could. I ran until I rounded the corner, and a bit dizzy from fasting, I sat down on a nearby bench. I turned the

book over. *Uncle Tom's Cabin*. Emma, I feel as though I am being swept up into something much bigger than myself. This is the book my relatives say is nothing but Yankee propaganda. I've heard them say that this book started the war and that it is filled with no-good ideas about freeing the slaves. An abolition handbook, they call it. Why would Miss Van Lew want me to read this book? Maybe she is a rebel against the Confederate cause. She doesn't fast. She's read this book. Who knows what she does at Libby Prison? What am I getting myself into?

Your friend,

Mollie

Washington, D.C.

August 1, 1861

Dear Mollie,

To answer your letter, I must take a risk in this one letter and speak plainly. BURN THIS LETTER after you read it.

You know how impulsive I can be. When I signed up for the army, I gave not a bit of thought to how in the world I was going to wash up and change clothes in a camp full of boys and men. I remember when the excitement of the send-off died down and we were settled on the train, I thought, *Oh, you've done it now. There is no way you're going to be able to keep this secret.*

I had no idea how long this charade might last, but war is kind to disguised soldiers. First of all, we don't often get out of our uniform. Sure we may take off our jacket, but we sleep, eat, ride, and march in our trousers. Some men take off their shirts, but I never do. No one has ever suspected that I have bandages binding up my chest underneath my shirt.

As for washing up, well, in the field the most any of us hope for is a handful of water splashed from a creek onto your face. Everyone does the same thing, so I don't stand out. We are all dusty and dirty and a chance to clean up doesn't come too often. The men don't seem to care that I'm not scruffy with my face full of whiskers. There are young boys in the camp who lied about their age to be able to fight. They haven't grown their beards yet either. Because of my size, they think I'm just a boy, and I don't say anything to change their minds.

I am so thankful for the city hospitals. When I am assigned to the hospitals in Washington, I can really clean up. There is more privacy in the hospitals here and because I often serve in more than one hospital, no one suspects if I clean up more frequently than the other field nurses do. I give myself a good scrubbing when I'm in a city hospital. After all, there's plenty of water, soap, and clean towels in the city hospital, and I don't know how long it will be before I'm out in the field again. So far, no one has noticed.

I always volunteer to go out in the city to seek donations from the civilians. They want those soldiers looking fine, so it gives me an additional reason to clean up. I enjoy meeting folks and hearing what they think of the war and slavery, so this is no chore for me.

As to the delicate question of tending to my bodily needs, that has been much harder. Many men relieve themselves in the pits for that purpose, but there are others who are more private. I've learned to wait long periods and to find private spots to take care of those needs. I try not to draw attention to myself, and I don't settle into any one routine. That way, no one expects me to be somewhere or do something and that helps me to guard my privacy.

It isn't easy, Mollie, but it *is* possible. I wonder if I'm the only female disguised as a soldier in these armies. I hear stories of wives who wanted to follow their men into battle—perhaps some of them did.

I don't blame you for asking such personal questions. I'd be curious too.

Your friend,

E

Richmond, Virginia

Dear E,

Sissy is back! She had gotten herself worked up thinking that maybe Lem was really all cut up, bloodied, or even missing an arm or leg and didn't want to frighten her. Sissy played that scenario over and over in her mind until it became real. Until she saw Lem with her own eyes, she wasn't going to be satisfied. Momma is very happy to have her back home. Sissy stitched all the way back on the train. Even Momma has to admit her handiwork is getting much better. Sissy says every stitch is filled with love for her Lem.

I took Sissy with me to Pizzini's to meet our friends. The price of a dish of ice cream is double what it was earlier this summer, so Sissy and I shared a bowl. All our friends wanted to know about Lem and Sissy's exciting trip to see him. Sissy, of course, exaggerated to create a better story.

Emily arrived with a new friend, Louly Wigfall. Her father used to be the senator from Texas when we were an undivided nation. Now he commands the First Texas Regiment that drills at a camp outside our city. Louly asked about Mrs. Pegram's school and my friends gladly filled her in on what a great school it is. I sat silent. Sissy suggested we walk over to see the new president's mansion, which all the girls wanted to do. Soon there was no more talk about Mrs. Pegram's school. I squeezed Sissy's hand under the table to thank her.

This afternoon, I went back to Miss Van Lew's to return the book she let me borrow. Emma, I read *Uncle Tom's Cabin* in one sitting. Then I read it again. I've been thinking about it for days. I can't get the story of Tom and Topsy out of my mind. I'm so angry at what happened to them. No wonder my Southern relatives never wanted me to read this book. It tells what slavery is really like, and you see the heart of these dear folks. But I wondered—was it made up by a Northerner to drum up support for the war?

When Miss Van Lew opened the door, I thrust the book into her hands, and said, "I read it all. Twice. Is it true?"

"It's a novel, Mollie, but Mrs. Stowe based the story on the lives of many slaves. As soon as I read it, I recognized many of the stories I've read. Would you like to read a story written by a slave who escaped his bondage thirty years ago and then helped other slaves escape to Canada?"

I nodded yes and Miss Van Lew motioned for me to follow her to the library. She selected a volume from the shelf and said, "This is my personal favorite. Josiah Henson is a remarkable man. Escaped slave and founder of a community of freed slaves in Canada. He met Queen Victoria in England, you know."

No, I did not know. The man sounded fascinating. I thanked Miss Van Lew and left with another treasure under my arm. I could not wait to get home to begin. Imagine my surprise when I opened the book and saw that Mrs. Stowe, the author of *Uncle Tom's Cabin*, had written the preface. She recommends this book to all who love the Lord Jesus Christ. She wrote that "whoever thought he would help Jesus, if he were sick or in prison, would help him now by helping the slaves, his afflicted and suffering children."

I raced through the book, putting it down only to weep and pray. This book affected me even more deeply than the first because Mr. Henson is a real person and his descriptions of all he suffered in slavery are so vivid. After reading his words about all he had gained from freedom, I felt as though I knew him. Emma, he's an amazing man, who lives now in your native country of Canada. I copied part of his story for you. Read these pages when you have time. They will astound you.

Your friend,

Mollie

Richmond, VA

AUGUST 22, 1861

Dear E,

Momma and I spent the morning at Robertson Hospital. None of the other Richmond ladies we know dress the wounds. The women, except for Momma, slip their handkerchiefs up to their noses as they read to the men or write letters for them. I suppose the smells offend their delicate sensibilities.

I remember the first time Miss Sally taught Momma and me how to dress a wound. I was so proud of Momma. You would've thought she'd done this for years. My efforts, on the other hand, were a much different story.

Miss Sally guided me to a young man who was just my age. He'd been hit by a minnie ball in his leg, and it was time to change the dressing. Miss Sally gently unwound the bandage, and as she got closer to the wound, I saw it was soaked in blood. I gripped the rail of the bed, for I was sure I would be sick. I smiled at the boy weakly, not wanting him to think I was shocked. Then as the bandage fell off, I stared at the gaping wound, packed with blood-soaked lint. Waves of nausea rushed over me.

I turned and ran outside and began to gulp in the fresh air. I thought about anything I could think about except that bloody wound. After a few minutes, I knew I had to go back in and try again. I didn't want to end up like one of those delicate Richmond ladies who say they help the wounded, but would faint if they saw the sight of blood.

By the time I got back inside, Miss Sally had removed the soiled lint and was beginning to pack the wound with fresh, clean lint. She turned to me and asked if I would like to help. *Like to? Not at all. Need to? Yes.*

I bit my lip hard to distract me. Miss Sally showed me how to gently place clean lint in the wound. She guided my hand the first

time and watched over me as I tried it myself. Her steady voice calmed me down, and I noticed that my hands had stopped shaking. Soon, she was showing me how to wrap the bandage around the wound. The young man said, "I knew you could do it." Momma beamed with pride. I was just glad I hadn't thrown up on the poor soldier.

Today, I stripped beds of soiled linens, remade them with fresh clean ones, and spent most of my time stirring a large vat of dirty linens in hot, soapy water. Miss Sally came by several times to make sure I was using enough soap. I tried not to think about the wounded soldiers at the hospital as my only duty today was the laundry. I dipped the sheets in and out of the warm water in the vat, and when the water turned pink from the bloodstained sheets, I had to rush outside for fresh air. I guess I am still not quite the strong nurse I hope to be. You on the other hand have the fortitude to do this all day long. I left in the early afternoon with my fingers pickled from the soapy water.

I asked Momma if I could visit Miss Van Lew again. Momma is not sure she approves of Miss Van Lew as a teacher, but then she sees how hungry I am for book learning. Momma feels bad that she can't send me to school, so she's agreed I can borrow books from Miss Van Lew's library. Momma said, "Just be careful not to borrow her ideas, child!" Momma may have her suspicions about Miss Van Lew's loyalties, but she has always believed in keeping an open mind. I think Daddy taught her that. Besides, Momma always told me "books are our friends." So long as I continue to help at Robertson Hospital, and keep quiet about what I am reading when I see our Richmond kin, Momma told me she will let me read these books.

I arrived at the Van Lew home with the book *Father Henson's Story* in my basket to return to her, and some flowers as a thank you. Just as I started to knock on the door, she opened it. Miss Van Lew had a basket on her arm and an armload of books. She seemed startled to see me.

"You're on your way out," I said. "Miss Van Lew, this was a wonderful book. I wept and wept. I want to know this man. I feel

like I do know this man. It's got me thinking, Miss Van Lew, about a lot of things."

"Child," she said, "I appreciate your enthusiasm, but if you are going to gab at me like that, would you mind helping me out? I see you have a basket there. Would you mind carrying some of these books and accompanying me? We can talk on the way."

"Where are you going?" I asked.

"To Libby Prison."

I pulled back. It's one thing to borrow literature from Miss Van Lew. It's quite another to assist her in her Federal activities.

"Oh, child, I'm not asking you to come inside with me. Just help me get the books down the hill. It's only four blocks. Not too far out of your way, is it?"

I thought about it a moment. What harm could it do? I'm helping a lady carry books. I'm not aiding the enemy, am I? Or am I?

But I wanted to talk more about Father Henson and abolition and fugitive slaves. Miss Van Lew was more than happy to tell me what she knew and explained all about something called the Underground Railroad. The walk to the prison was much too short.

Miss Van Lew said she would not be long. She simply wanted to leave these books with the warden. She used to be able to visit with the men, but now that the Northern army is on the move, she's not allowed to speak to them personally. I decided to wait for her. I wanted to learn more about the Underground Railroad.

When she came back, she had armloads of books that the prisoners had returned to her. She briefly looked through them and placed some of them in her basket and some in mine. Then we trudged up the hill to her home. When we got to her home, she took both baskets to her library and then returned with mine, which now contained a few more books she wanted me to read.

She gave me some biscuits with butter and a tall glass of milk. I looked at her in surprise for eggs, milk, and butter are in short supply. "I have a farm," she said. As she spread butter on my biscuit and handed it to me, she continued, "It's not too far from the city.

When we freed all our slaves, some of them stayed to work the farm—for wages. They are kind enough to bring eggs and milk to Mother and me."

When it was time to go, I turned to Miss Van Lew and said, "You don't seem like a spy to me."

Miss Van Lew laughed and said, "And what, pray tell, does a spy look like?"

I fumbled for a few moments, and then said, "Oh, I don't know—sinister, evil perhaps. Anyway, all my Richmond kin say you and your mother are spies. I overheard one lady when we were sewing say that it was not what you took into the prisons that bothered them, it was what you brought out."

"Hmmm. Well, you were here with me today. What did I bring out?"

"Just books, Ma'am."

"Yes," said Miss Van Lew in a hushed voice, "but those books might be filled with secrets."

My eyes widened. "Really?" I said.

Miss Van Lew laughed and shooed me out the door, telling me to come back anytime for more books. All the way home, I had to wonder ... were they?

Your friend,

Mollie

Washington, D.C.

SEPTEMBER 5, 1861

Dear Mollie,

This is not good. Not good at all. The Rebel flag is flying on Munson's Hill, in plain sight of the Federal Capitol. President Lincoln ordered General McClellan to take command of the Army of the Potomac. This army's in a sad state. For weeks, stragglers sneaked along through the mud trying to find their regiments.

The extraordinary march from Bull Run, through rain, mud, and shame, did more to fill the hospitals than the battle itself. The soldiers are sick with measles, dysentery, and typhoid fever. There are not enough surgeons or nurses to care for them.

Some of our men are in grave states of delirium. I checked on one soldier, John Coles, throughout the night. He would sleep for a while, but then a vivid recollection of the battlefield would come to his mind. He'd sit up in bed, and load and fire his pretend musket over and over again. When we tell him the enemy has retreated, he still wants to pursue them. Throwing his arms around wildly, he shouts, "Come on men and fight while there is one Rebel left in Virginia!"

There is so much suffering, but I cannot go among the patients with a long, sad face or intimate by word or look that their case is hopeless. Cheerfulness is my motto. I've noticed that if a man thinks he is a helpless case, then very often he is.

It looks like I'm going to be here in Washington for a while. Is there any chance you could come to visit your great aunt ... and me?

Your friend,

E

Richmond, Virginia

SEPTEMBER 30, 1861

Dear E,

You should have seen Miss Sally today! Robertson Hospital is the Richmond ladies' favorite place to visit. They say they come to volunteer, but none of them has chased any dirt in years. Their servants care for their dresses, their dishes, and their floors. They really don't come to work, but rather to be able to say that they worked. Miss Sally has no patience for those who won't roll up their sleeves and met the ladies at the door today with aprons, rags, and a list of chores so long, I wonder if we'll ever see them again.

Sissy says she would come and help, but it makes her queasy to see all the wounded men there. She is not so worried anymore about Lemuel because his unit has only seen a small skirmish or two since the big battle at Manassas. She tries to get away to see him when she can.

It seems like things are quiet on both sides now. Perhaps it will stay that way.

The Richmond ladies may adore Miss Sally as our very own Florence Nightingale, but they despise Miss Van Lew's offers of help to the Federal prisoners. Mrs. Adams whispered to Momma today at the hospital that Miss Van Lew continues to bring the Federal prisoners books, food, stationery, and good cheer. Does that make her evil? These ladies seem to think so. I think not. I think she is courageous.

It takes courage to hold views of the minority at a time when everyone's words and actions are watched so closely. If she chooses to use her funds to help the Federals have more comforts in prison, isn't that as righteous as Miss Sally using her funds to help the Confederate wounded?

The government approved my pass for two weeks in Washington. Next week I visit Great Auntie and you!

Your friend,

Mollie

Washington, D.C.

OCTOBER 12, 1861

Dear Mollie,

Félicitations! I hope you've recovered from the excitement of our time together yesterday. I should never have let you talk me into it!

For a girl who had never been on a horse before, you did quite well with old Ginger. She's steady when she pulls our ambulance. I think she was gentle enough for you. Good thing too, with all the excitement of our journey. Too bad you're not free to share your adventure with your friends at Pizzini's. They'd be horrified at best and, at worst, turn you in as a spy!

If only you hadn't said you wanted to see the pickets! I bet you never expected those pickets would begin to send volleys of minnie balls across to each other just as we arrived. When the Rebels opened fire, it was just a miracle that we were able to reach cover in time.

I think your great uncle would have had my hide if he'd known what we were doing. If he'd seen that minnie ball strike the rail right behind your head, he'd have gotten me booted out of the army for sure.

So, how's that for your introduction to my secret life! Want to join up? Would you sign up with the blues or the grays?

I'm on duty the next few days, but I'll try to get away early next week so we can talk. Would you like to see the rotunda of the Capitol? I can show you around.

Your friend,

Æ

Richmond, Virginia

OCTOBER 20, 1861

Dear Frank,

Made it home safely. Just wanted you to know. Much to do and can't write now. More later.

Your friend,

Mollie

Emma, I hope it worked. Did you have to heat this letter long before the writing appeared? You're a clever girl, to have thought of this secret way to write. I never knew that soda and water could be used for invisible writing! Great Auntie continues to praise her private courier as exceedingly trustworthy, but the danger increases. We'd heard that both governments are opening letters now, especially the ones that go between the South and the North. With our invisible ink we can speak more freely.

I thought about our talk all the way back on the train to Richmond. You're one amazing girl, Emma Edmonds. I'm proud of you. Nothing convinced me more of the rightness of what you are doing than when I went to the hospital with you and saw how the soldiers respect you (or rather, Frank). They talked of your compassion and your bravery and what a skilled horseman you are. I am proud to be your friend. I'm so glad I got to see you in action.

I know you are certain the boys in your company don't know. I heard them call you their "little woman" at the hospital, but you said that is because your boots are so small. You clearly have their respect as a soldier, so I assume they're simply teasing you for being smaller than most of them.

I puzzled and puzzled about it on the train, but I realize that just as I'm used to moving a certain way to avoid bumping into things with my hoop skirt or catching the angel sleeves of my dress in the fire of a candle, you are accustomed to wearing pants, chopping wood, riding horses, shooting a gun, and holding your own with young Canadian boys: hunting, fishing, or racing horses across open fields and farmlands. Your body is used to moving without encumbrances. Mine is used to living with them. No wonder the Yankee uniform is a relief to you.

You get to ride a horse every day. You have a pistol in your belt. And yet, when you enlisted, the captain assigned you the duties of a field nurse, to work side by side with surgeons in saving lives and relieving suffering. It was as if God knew exactly where he wanted you with your big heart of compassion and your commitment to tend men's souls as well as their wounds — and he prepared you from childhood for the task.

I want to make a difference too. But how?

Your friend,

Mollie

Richmond, Virginia

NOVEMBER 1, 1861

Dear Emma,

Miss Sally Tompkins is now *Captain* Sally Tompkins, Captain in the Army of the Confederate States of America. Aha, Emma Edmonds! You're not the only female in the army. And Miss Sally is an *officer!* So which side is more forward thinking now, Miss Emma? Is it the North with its token disguised private in the Second Michigan Regiment or the South with its publicly proclaimed female captain?

Even Great Uncle Chester is harrumphing about this one! He, the great champion of women's rights, doesn't know what to say. I think he just wishes the Northern army had done it first!

The Confederate government ordered all private hospitals closed. The government couldn't locate its wounded soldiers scattered in so many homes and churches. You mentioned you had the same problem after the Battle of Manassas. (I know, you Federals call it the Battle of Bull Run.)

Anyway, when Miss Sally got wind of the planned closings, she went to President Davis and spread out all her neatly-kept hospital records. She told him that no other hospital sends such a high percentage of soldiers back into active duty than does Robertson Hospital. President Davis couldn't change the order so he had to think of a way around it. He offered to make her an army officer, which would make her hospital an official Confederate army hospital. She willingly took the commission. Momma says that Captain Sally may have accepted the rank of Captain from the government, but she does not accept the pay. Captain Sally pays for all the medicines and supplies herself.

Well, in my opinion, with or without the official title, she has always run this place like a regiment. Clean blankets, clean sheets, clean clothes are the order of the day. When I volunteer, I help as much with the dressing of the beds as I do with the dressing of the wounds. Captain Sally simply does not tolerate dirt.

All the men love Captain Sally, as they call her. Her care for their bodies is only surpassed by her care for their souls. But, she can be tough. When one soldier decided he was well enough to sneak out for some time in the city, she took away his clothes so he couldn't escape again until he was truly well.

Your friend,

Mollie

Washington, D.C.

NOVEMBER 5, 1861

Dear Mollie,

You should see the companies of men in full-dress parade. It's a far cry from the panicked army that fled Bull Run. When the time for action comes, we'll be ready. James came by the hospital today after the drills. He said the men are getting restless, anxious for battle. He was restless himself and I put him to work helping me with the patients. There are less fevers now, but many of the men in our hospitals suffer from disease. I'm very careful, but my duties require me to be close to these sick men. I pray I don't get sick. I can't be discovered, and if I am confined to bed, I fear I will be found out.

I volunteered to take your "Greats" to view a skirmish at the pickets, but they declined. Your great uncle says he prefers stitching men up to watching them blown asunder and your great aunt nearly fainted when I suggested it.

Thank you for understanding why I chose to enlist. I suppose because I know what it's like to be in bondage to fear—in my case, fear of my own father—I have sympathies for the slave. Even more, dear friend, I cannot reconcile slavery with what is taught in the New Testament. Enlisting was the best way I knew to do my part for this wonderful country that adopted me and gave me shelter.

Your friend,

Emma

Richmond, Virginia

Dear Emma,

I visited Miss Van Lew again. And, again we took books down to Libby Prison. I carried buttermilk and fresh eggs from Miss Van Lew's farm. She gave them to the warden. She keeps the guards on her side with sweets and fresh food from her farm, and they continue to let her bring books into the prisons.

They examined the books, both when she took them in and when she brought them out. They turned them upside down and shook them. They flipped through the pages. I guess they thought letters or secret messages would fall out. But, if Miss Van Lew is a spy, I know she's smarter than that. If there are secrets hidden in those books, they're truly hidden.

However, when she came out of the prison, I noticed that she flipped through the books as well, and carefully placed some of the books in her basket and the remainder into mine. I thought about it all the way back to her house. It was a warm day, and we didn't talk much as we trudged up the hill to her home with our heavy loads.

She gave me her usual treat of biscuit, butter, and milk once the books were put away. Then she brought back my basket filled this time with several new books.

"You are a very fast reader, Miss Mollie. Can you carry all these books home today?" I lifted the basket and assured her I could. I asked her for one of the books we had taken from the prison, pretending that I was interested in its topic. She seemed surprised, but went back to the library to get it and added it to my basket.

I hurried home. If Miss Van Lew was getting secret messages from the prisoners in the books, I knew they weren't messages on paper. Unless they're written with a special ink, like ours are.

I heated the book in the oven at a low temperature for a few minutes. I could hardly wait for it to cool. I flipped through the book forward and backward and found not one single word had appeared. I was very disappointed. Well, maybe she's not a spy after all. Or then, maybe she has another way to get messages out of these books.

Your friend,

Mollie

Washington, D.C.

DECEMBER 25, 1861

Dear Mollie,

Joyeaux Noël!

Today I went to church, and it was a welcome reminder of why I am doing what I am doing. There were many soldiers in uniform in the pews. The rumors that we'll be marching and fighting again bring many into the church to get right with God.

No roast turkey today, but our rations included some of the good gifts of the citizens of this great city. A dear lady slipped me a bit of tea as I left the church. I do wish I could share it with you. No sugar though.

Your friend,

Emma

Richmond, Virginia

DECEMBER 26, 1861

Dear Emma,

Such a somber Christmas. At church on Christmas Eve, everyone still called out "Merry Christmas" and "God bless you," but hushed conversations about who has heard what from whom in the field quickly followed. Fathers, brothers, and sons were all missing from the Christmas Eve service. I thought of you, dear friend, and wished you all God's love and protection in these perilous times.

Momma has decided to take in boarders. Sissy and I share a room now, and Momma has taken the little room in the back of our house so that she can rent out the front two bedrooms that look out over the city. The mother is nice company for Momma. They have a boy, William, age ten and a girl, Mary, who is fifteen. And yes, Mary will attend Mrs. Pegram's school. If I sound envious, that's because I am.

Mary's family stayed at their home in Alexandria until it was overrun by the Federal soldiers. As first, all they did was take their fruit and vegetables, and their chickens and cows. But when Confederate soldiers made several raids on the railroad near their home, the Federal general ordered all the woods within ten miles of the railroad track to be cut down. Mary's mother begged the captain to leave a few trees around their house for shade, but the soldiers swiftly cut what few trees were left. A few weeks later, their home was confiscated for Federal headquarters. They had one day to pack up to leave.

Mary and her mother hid as many of their valuables as they could. Mary made mortar out of the clay, sand, and lime in her basement and used it to brick up the silver and jewelry into the base of the chimney. She darkened up the fresh mortar with soot from the fireplace. Her brother hid things under floorboards and in the

attic behind the eaves. Mary told me that right before they left, her mother walked around the house and touched furniture, pictures, and books, as if she was saying good-bye.

Momma is happy about the boarders. If truth be told, we can use the money. With the tightening blockade by the North, prices are skyrocketing. Salt is $1.40 a sack and apples are $20 a barrel. Our Christmas turkey cost us $4.00! Momma says she is going to make it last a week with turkey hash, turkey soup, and turkey fritters.

We didn't have our usual Christmas pies and ice cream. Ice cream is up to $9 a quart! I'm glad it's not summer or trips to Pizzini's would be out of the question. Maybe Sissy was right to hoard her sugar. Tea is a luxury and coffee is nonexistent. Momma misses her coffee, and Sissy and I miss our tea. A cup of hot tea would be so lovely now. With sugar!

Sissy used most of her hoarded sugar in a pound cake for Lem for Christmas. She wrapped it with paper and ribbon and sprigs of holly and put it, along with four pairs of socks, a woolen scarf, and a jar of pickles, in a box to take to Lem. I donated the socks. Sissy's stitching has improved, but she still cannot create patterns with her knitting. All she can do is knit a straight row, and she has not yet mastered one sock.

One night a few weeks ago, Sissy threw down her knitting in frustration and cried out that she's a failure as a wife. Twisting her hair over and over, she sat there, miserable, staring at me as I worked my knitting needles on which hung a perfect sock.

Momma suggested Sissy make Lem a nice long, straight scarf. Momma, knowing Sissy is such a romantic, told her it would comfort Lem to have a scarf worked with her love to keep him warm in the winter. "Feet are for marching, but necks are for hugging," said Momma knowingly. Sissy threw her arms around Momma and was soon happily clicking along with her needles again. It took Sissy forever to knit the four-foot scarf, but Momma was glad she had something to do to keep her from twisting.

My fingers can knit and purl in their sleep, I suspect. And yarn, my dear friend! Oh my, is it expensive. There will be no cotton for dresses in the spring either. We hear the Southerners are burning cotton rather than let the Federals get it. I imagine the dress I wear today may be worn a great deal before the war is over, and may ultimately be worn out.

By the way, enclosed is your belated Christmas present. Two pairs of my best work—socks for your "little woman" feet. Momma and I took our homemade gifts to the soldiers at Robertson Hospital. Captain Sally was most appreciative, but it was the soap Momma made for her that thrilled her the most.

Your friend—especially
at Christmas,

Mollie

Washington, D.C.

January 5, 1862

Dear Mollie,

Dear friend, *merci*! These socks are a most welcome gift—especially with all the drilling we've been doing in this cold, snowy, miserable winter. They are on my feet now as I write. We know we're ready for battle. Each soldier knows it. Yet all we do is wait. After the pitiful showing at Manassas last summer, the boys want to show the Confederates they can fight. There is much grumbling going on in the ranks. If we do not have orders soon, I fear we may have deserters.

Yesterday, we received news of the Union capture of Nashville, the capital of Tennessee. When the announcement was made, the men started calling out, "Forward to Richmond. On to Richmond." We are desperate to be part of the reclaiming of the Rebel states into the Union, yet we are stuck here in Washington—drilling, drilling, drilling.

The president and Mrs. Lincoln have suffered greatly. Their son, twelve-year-old Willie, died last Thursday from a fever. I wonder if it is typhoid that claims so many lives here. I must admit that typhoid, more than minnie balls, scares me, Mollie. It's just as much an enemy and much less predictable. Catching that disease would land me in the hospital, and I'd be discovered for sure then. It's a horrible disease. With the cold weather, many more men have gotten sick. Some have died.

James is a tremendous help to us. Although he's a soldier training for battle, he comes to the hospitals when he's off duty. He moves among the wounded with ease. The men are glad for his comfort and his laughter. He reads to them from the Bible, and jokes with the boys to keep up their spirits. Things are always brighter when he is around. For me too.

Your friend,

Emma

Richmond, Virginia

JANUARY 6, 1862

Dear Emma,

People say Southerners want to choose their own way of life. President Davis told the Confederate Congress: "Liberty is always won where there exists the unconquerable will to be free." But doesn't the slave have an unconquerable will to be free? Isn't it the North who speaks for them?

Emma, you've committed every resource, skill, and talent you have to what you believe. I, on the other hand, don't know what I can do. Knitting socks day in and out or changing sheets on the beds of wounded soldiers is not my idea of contributing to the war effort. I want to make a difference. I wish Daddy were still here to talk through these things with me.

Charlie very faithfully comes by each week to read the papers with me. He reminds me he will soon be fifteen and then he's off to join his brother's regiment. I remind him his mother said sixteen is the magic age. He continues to practice with his drumsticks on his nonexistent drum. He says he'll be the best drummer the Confederates have ever seen. Wherever Charlie is, his drumsticks are with him. Momma forbids him to rat-ta-tat-tat on our table, but she suffered through his practicing on the railing of our veranda last summer. I don't mind. I understand how Charlie feels.

With the nursing at Robertson Hospital, until the last few weeks I had very little time to read the books Miss Van Lew lent to me. I wanted to get back to see Miss Van Lew as soon as possible, but I needed an excuse—the books. I couldn't pretend to read them, because she asks me lots of questions about each book I read. She won't let me get away with parroting what I've heard others say.

Mostly, I wanted to try to figure out how she is getting messages in and out of Libby Prison. I am certain that she is. But today was not to be one of those days. We didn't go to Libby Prison.

I made a great pretense of wanting to see her library so that I could look through many of her books, but I saw nothing out of the ordinary.

One of her freed slaves who works on the farm, Nelson, visited with a basket of eggs. He disappeared into the kitchen for a few minutes and then he left. I went into the kitchen for another glass of milk (Miss Van Lew has told me to make myself at home), and I noticed one egg set off to the side on a plate. The others were in the basket. When I asked Miss Van Lew about it, she looked surprised, and then said, "Never you mind, Miss Mollie. It's just a rotten one, that's all."

I don't think so, Emma. There is something about that egg. There is something about Nelson. I could tell by the way he raised his eyebrows at Miss Van Lew when he motioned to me. She had whispered for him not to worry, but I heard it all. Something is definitely going on here.

Your friend,

Mollie

Richmond, Virginia

JANUARY 15, 1862

Dear Emma,

On to Richmond! Obviously, we all know that Richmond is the great prize the Federals seek, but that's the last thing I want to hear.

Sissy and I met an interesting new refugee today, Constance Cary. Constance does not believe in slavery; yet she is a Confederate. Constance told us that her grandfather freed his slaves years ago and made sure that each of his freed slaves learned a trade at his expense so that they could support themselves.

A few years ago, Constance spent three years here in Richmond at the boarding school of Monsieur Hubert Pierre Lefebvre. It was there, she said, that she became convinced that slave service did not create the energy of the body or the independence of ideas that she had been taught to value since she was a little girl. Most of the girls from the deepest southern states who attended school with her had never put on a shoe or stocking for themselves. Can you imagine that? Slave girls attended to their every need. Constance thinks that becoming used to others doing for you creates a laziness of mind and heart.

Constance said her family and their friends didn't want Virginia to secede from the Union, but when Virginia did, they chose to remain loyal. She used to shop in Washington and visit friends. She says it is impossible for her to think of that city as the enemy. I cannot either, for it contains my dear great auntie and my best friend.

Your friend,

Mollie

Richmond, Virginia

FEBRUARY 22, 1862

Dear Emma,

I haven't heard from you in such a long time. I'm worried. Are you all right? I've gotten three letters from Great Auntie, but nothing from you. Please write soon.

Today Mr. Jefferson Davis became the official president of the Confederacy. Thanks to Constance's uncle, we girls viewed the festivities from the galleries of the Capitol and avoided the drenching rain that fell on the crowds. Later, we went together to the president's mansion.

While we were waiting to go inside, Constance introduced us to Hetty and Jennie, her cousins from Baltimore, Maryland. When Maryland did not join the southern states, they found themselves in a Federal city. That didn't stop Hetty. She took a Confederate banner that had been smuggled through the lines to her, and unfurled it from a window of her home. The Federals took it down and warned her to leave Baltimore or suffer immediate arrest, so the two sisters, along with their brother, ran the blockade, carrying drugs for the Confederate hospitals hidden in their birdcage skirts. They also wore new shirts and pants under their dresses for their friends who had enlisted in the Confederacy. Hetty and Jennie laughed to remember how heavy-laden they were with their bottles of quinine and several layers of clothing. Imagine that, Emma!

Fearlessness must run in her family. When the army came to take over her elderly aunt's home in Alexandria, she refused to leave. The Federal officer informed them that they must move and that a war-carriage (that's what Constance calls it—it's really an army ambulance) stood waiting for them at the door. Her aunt positively refused to move. She sat there defying them, fire in her eyes, iron in her veins, until two soldiers lifted her, chair and all, and carried her out of the house and put her in the ambulance.

We waited nearly two hours to get into the mansion, but it seemed like two minutes. Each story the girls told topped the last one. Nothing that exciting ever happens to me.

I was so caught up with Hetty's story that I hadn't realized we had made it into the mansion, down the hall, and into the drawing room where President and Mrs. Davis greeted the visitors. I know I should have been watching where I was going, but my feet were going one way while my eyes were glued to these brave girls, and I was hanging on every word.

Suddenly, I bumped into President Davis himself—stumbling hard and catching myself from falling by grabbing his arm. My face burned hot, and I felt like disappearing into the velvet curtains. Mrs. Davis touched my arm and said, "My dear, we are all leaning on him these days, aren't we?" The president laughed, and I didn't feel quite so stupid. Next time, I'll watch where I'm going!

Your friend,

Mollie

Richmond, Virginia

FEBRUARY 24, 1862

Dear Emma,

Still no word from you. Emma, you must write! I'm worried. I've asked Great Auntie to check on you (or Private Frank Thompson, that is).

President Davis declared today a day of prayer and fasting for the Confederacy. All the girls are making a big show of going without food and attending services at St. Paul's where the president attends.

Charlie stopped by and spread the newspaper out on the kitchen table. "The paper says here, Mollie," he began to read, "that there is a strong and gallant band of Union men in Richmond willing and anxious to welcome the old flag. Hmmm. Says here that Union ladies are very numerous, and they spend their money to help the Federals in Richmond's prisons and hospitals."

I immediately thought of Miss Van Lew. "Does it say who these men and women are, Charlie?" I asked.

"Nope. Just tells us we better watch out here because this group of traitors is some three thousand persons strong."

I had no idea there were that many people in Richmond who favored the North. I hurried Charlie as he read through the rest of the paper. He was willing to leave soon enough because it was clear I would offer him no food or drink on this fast day. When he left, I put on my cloak and hat and slipped out the back and made my way to Grace Street.

Miss Van Lew welcomed me inside. I'd been in such a hurry to leave, I forgot to bring the books. Miss Van Lew offered me tea and a biscuit. Nelson was there again, and he eyed me suspiciously. He tipped his hat at Miss Van Lew and told her the eggs were on her counter. I was desperate to take a look at the eggs, but Miss Van Lew kept me in the formal dining room.

"Do you know what the paper said today, Miss Van Lew?" She sipped her tea, waiting for me to continue. "It said there are three thousand traitors in our city ready to welcome the Union flag."

"Hmmm ... three thousand, you say?"

"Yes, and it said that there are Union ladies who tend the Federals in prison and hospitals."

"Mollie, tell me what you think. Is it a crime to visit the Federals in prison or help them when wounded?"

I remembered the Bible verse I read this morning about visiting prisoners. *When you do it unto the least of these you have done it unto me.*

"Well, no, but perhaps it is a crime to take something from one of the wounded Federals and use it to help the Federal cause?"

"Perhaps, but what if it is freely given? Given by one who is incapable of using it himself, but who would ... that is, if he could."

I knew what she was saying. If she is bringing secrets out of Libby Prison, she is bringing out what the men want her to know and want her to use on their behalf. I am more convinced than ever that she is a spy and that she conducts her activities at Libby Prison.

"Mollie, think about it this way. Suppose you were nursing a wounded Confederate soldier at Robertson Hospital, and he wanted you to pass on a message to his mother back home about his whereabouts and what he had seen and heard before he was wounded. Would you do it?"

"Of course."

"What if that same soldier had another message that he needed to go to another? He offers it to you because he cannot take it himself. You are now his hands and feet to accomplish that which the bars of the prison or the wounds of battle make impossible for him to do himself. Would that be a criminal act if the message to his mother was not?"

It made sense. Too much sense perhaps. "Miss Van Lew, if you're suggesting what I think you're suggesting, it's treason."

Nelson burst into the room before she could answer. He motioned to Miss Van Lew and she quickly rose. "You must leave

now, Mollie." She ushered me outside before I could find out what was going on. I thought I heard a door open in the back but I strained to see someone, anything. There is activity in that house. Secret activity. I just know it.

Your friend,

Mollie

Washington, D.C.

MARCH 1, 1862

Dear Mollie,

By now, your great aunt has probably written to you of her visit to me. She found me delirious and watched over by my good friend James. I don't know what made me feel worse—the high fever or the fear I said something in my delirium that gave me away. I haven't asked James yet. I'm too afraid to find out what I may have said.

I was on duty one night very late. I'd just finished seeing patients and was labeling medicine vials in the cabinet of our stockroom when I grabbed the counter and crashed to the floor. The medicine vials came with me, and James told me the nurses said it made quite a clatter, especially so late at night when the wards were quiet.

All I know is that days later, I am much better. I can only hope I haven't been found out. I've had no visits from the army officer in charge of this hospital. Every time someone turns the corner toward my bed, my heart races. Have I been found out? Is this the officer who will discharge me with dishonor? It's always been a nurse or one of the men in our regiment who've come to cheer me up. I study each of them, but they seem none the wiser. The doctor says I can go back on duty tomorrow. The sooner I can get back to my regular routine, the sooner I'll stop worrying about being kicked out of the army.

James seems quiet though. I wonder what I said. Oh, Molly, I am so afraid he is suspicious of my true identity. He seems different. Distant. But I dare not ask him about it. I didn't realize until now how much serving in the army means to me. I just want everything to be back to normal.

Your friend,

Emma

Washington, D.C.

MARCH 10, 1862

Dear Mollie,

I'm fit as a fiddle and glad to be back. No visits from officers. James hasn't said anything, but once I caught him looking at me kind of funny.

Now for my great news! I've been appointed by Colonel Poe to be the regiment's mail carrier. It's a wonderful job, especially now that there are no battles. Nothing delights me more than being the bearer of a letter or package from home. I know the men of Company F quite well, but this job will let me get to know the men in the other companies of our regiment. The only thing is that I won't see James as much, but he was thrilled for me when he learned of my appointment.

Better yet, it means I can be in the saddle most of the day. You know how I love to ride. I enjoy my hospital work, but I miss the wind in my face as I gallop across fields on a good horse.

There's just this one problem. I learned this week that each side considers it a great success to steal the opposite side's mail. There may be posts or messages of great interest to the other army. The last mail carrier was knocked out for hours, and when he awoke his mail pouch was gone. I wonder if I'll be able to get any sleep while carrying the mail? I bet the sound of my heart pounding while I rest will be enough to keep me alert!

Your friend,

Emma

Richmond, Virginia

MARCH 12, 1862

Dear Emma,

Emma Edmonds, you scared me to death! I'm so glad to hear you're better now. Great Auntie gave me a full report. The only thing she said that you mumbled in your feverish delirium while she was visiting was something like "you can't find out" and "no, I'm not." I know what you meant by that, but Great Auntie wasn't alarmed. Do you think you said something else while James was there? Now, stay well, good friend, and don't scare me like that again!

President Davis has declared martial law in Richmond. The army rules the city now. Two dozen people have been arrested for Union loyalties. Some people say they are spies. No women have been arrested. Yet.

The Greats have decided to move Great Auntie to Baltimore. Washington's become more like a fort, and she misses civilian life. Great Auntie made all the necessary arrangements with the courier to make sure our letters get to each other. She says we're to trust her courier. He's loyal to the Union and able to move about freely in Richmond. Letter paper is becoming increasingly scarce. I'm glad I purchased a supply for our letters long ago when the price was much lower and paper more plentiful.

Sissy is a bundle of nerves as word has come that Lem's unit is preparing for battle. She's taken off again to be near him. I miss her.

Your friend,

Mollie

Camp of Company E, near Hampton, Virginia

MARCH 29, 1862

Dear Mollie,

We finally got our orders. "On to Richmond!" the boys shouted.
But it's done nothing but rain. We march in the rain. We sleep
in the rain. We try to cook in the rain—an effort that is made
more difficult due to the lack of food. We had two days' rations for
marching, but it's been three days since we camped, and the mules
pulling the food wagons became stuck in the mud days ago. No rest.
My feet hurt and my stomach is knotted up with hunger pains. Last
night, I was so hungry, I took the piece of rainsoaked hardtack that
James discarded and gobbled it down when he wasn't looking. It
was a sodden mush of flour, but at least that sodden mess fooled my
stomach into thinking it had nourishment.

James and I went to houses to ask for food. They gave us
bacon, biscuits, pies, and corn bread. When we returned to camp,
we smelled the smoke of steak cooking. Someone found a farmer's
cow and shot it and, as quick as lightning, had it roasting on the
fire. This is exactly the kind of behavior you wrote about, Mollie.
But I ask you to consider how men who have been marching for
days without food might look at a cow in a field? They do not
ask permission. They just take. I'm not saying it is right. I just
understand why they are doing it. And, I admit, it tasted really
good. James and I added our stash of food to the meal and, before
long, the soldiers with us roared with laughter as they told jokes.
Yes, spirits lift when stomachs are full.

While we were out calling on homes today for food, James said
he was glad I seemed to be completely recovered. I didn't want to
talk much about being sick though, so I tried to change the subject.
"Yessiree, feeling great now," I said. "How much food do you think

we can get from this next town?" James jogged a bit ahead of me, then turned around and stood in my path. I stopped short, and looked him right in the eye. After all, when you have something to hide, perhaps it is best to act like you have nothing to hide.

"Frank, I gotta ask you something." He paused, and then asked, "Who's Emma?"

I froze. "Emma?"

"It's something you said when you were sick. I can't rightly put it all together."

"What did I say?"

"You said, 'Don't want James to know.' Then a few minutes later, you said, 'It's Emma.' So, who's Emma and why don't you want me to know about her? Is she your gal back home? How come you've never mentioned her?"

I rubbed my palms on my trousers and then tipped my hat back and scratched my head. I had to think. *He thinks Emma is my girlfriend. But he's wondering why I've never mentioned her.* So I told him the truth—at least most of it.

"James, Emma is my closest relative. She's had a rough life. Her father was a cruel man, and she had to leave home at her mother's insistence for her safety. She worked for her mother's friend at her hat shop for a while in Canada, but then her father caught up with her and she was on the run again. I haven't seen Emma in a long, long time. Sometimes I fear I'll never see her again."

That seemed to satisfy him, and he returned to his jovial self. We walked on to the next town, and he didn't follow up with any other questions. I think Emma is safe for now. And so is Frank.

I imagine this little town of about five hundred homes used to be quite lovely, but all the houses were burned by order of Confederate General Magruder. You see, it's not only the Federals who destroy homes and trees. I suppose the Rebels wanted a clearer view of our Fortress Monroe that is three miles away. Or maybe it was because the Yorktown road passes directly through the middle. Either way, it is sad to see the burned bricks that used to house families.

Last night, there was a great ruckus at one o'clock in the morning. We left our tents to see what was happening. About forty slaves fell to their knees with hands lifted up to heaven shouting thanks to God and to the soldiers for their deliverance. They had made their way through the Rebel lines to the Federal picket line. No sooner had their feet touched Federal soil, than they fell on their knees and shouted, "Glory. Glory to God!"

The men and women and children gathered together in a group, praying, singing, and shouting praises. We had a real camp meeting, loud and joyful, as these folks rejoiced. Soldiers brought out coffee, meat, and bread, and built a huge fire since these poor folks were soaked to the bone. James distributed blankets.

James told me later, "There is no sweeter sound to me than the sound of a person tasting freedom for the first time." Mollie, that's why I'm fighting in this war. That's why the Union has to win. I think you know it too.

Your friend,

Emma

Camp near Yorktown, Virginia

April 3, 1862

Dear Mollie,

It's a great relief to leave that old mud hole we had for our camp. We've had a number of skirmishes and cannon balls and minnies whiz over us, but no casualties. We prepared the hospital and laid down planks into makeshift floors in the hospital tents. But once again, we find ourselves waiting—waiting for battle.

This week, I rode twenty-five miles over muddy roads to Fortress Monroe to pick up the first mail in more than a week. At night, I would lay down by my horse to sleep, but all I could think about was the news that last week a soldier carrying his regiment's mail was killed on the same road I'd just traveled to get the army's mail. One of the benefits of being small was that I tucked myself and my mail pouch into pockets of brush and covered myself over at night. I thought this was a grand plan, until the third night on the road.

I'd covered myself in a crevice with dry brush. It was not so thick that I couldn't breathe, but thick enough to hide me and the mail pouch. I'd just drifted off to sleep with the mail pouch underneath me and my horse tied up to a tree not too far away. A sharp crack of a branch breaking jerked me back awake. I couldn't see anything, but the sound of the footsteps got louder. I held my breath and sweat poured down my face as I tried to tell whether the steps were moving towards me or towards my horse. Finally, the horse whinnied, and I knew some rascal was trying to mount him and ride him away. I rolled out of my ditch, grabbed my gun, and raced over to the horse just as the soldier had untied her rope.

"You've got five seconds to get out of here," I shouted and leveled my gun at his chest. He reached for his pistol, and I fired. I shot his pistol right out of his hand. That rascal started running as fast as he could. I grabbed my mail pouch, jumped up on my horse, and hightailed it out of there. For the next two nights, I didn't sleep at

all and jumped at every sound in the woods. I was never so happy as to return to camp. I fell into my camp bed and slept for thirteen hours straight.

Tonight James and I decided to visit a community of fugitive slaves near our camp. The men load and unload the military ships that arrive here and the women wash and cook, all for wages now that they are in Federally controlled lands.

I cannot describe the joy of these men and women at being liberated from bondage. There may not be much book learning among these slaves, but oh, Mollie, they are deeply knowledgeable about the way of salvation. James and I read to them from the Bible. I wish they could read it for themselves. Yet, many had long passages of the Bible memorized.

Then, one by one, they began to share their life stories, the terror of their time in slavery, the fears suffered after they escaped, the pain of leaving behind those who were dear to them, and the dreams they shared for a life of freedom. Toward the end, one man stood up and said, "I tell you, my brothers, that the good Lord has borne with this here slavery a long time with great patience. But now he can't bear it any longer; and he has said to the people of the North 'Go and tell the slave holders to let the people go, that they may serve me.'"

Many of the soldiers who were drawn to the meeting by the shouts of praise and the beautiful voices lifted up in singing, turned aside lest a fellow soldier see a tear slide down his cheek. Strong men with tender hearts. Men need a reason to fight, Mollie, and there is no greater reason than the freeing of a slave, a man, a brother.

Your friend,

Emma

Richmond, Virginia

APRIL 6, 1862

Dear Emma,

At church this morning, a soldier marched to the front and announced that three trainloads of soldiers who had been fighting in the valley were expected in an hour, and they hadn't eaten in days. Emma, you should see what happens when Confederate men need food. Confederate women are equal to the task!

All afternoon, hundreds of ladies and their daughters, with aprons covering their Sunday best, marched up and down Main Street and Broad Street carrying platters piled high with bacon, cabbage, and corn pones. They carried jugs of sorghum and Confederate lemonade (vinegar and water since you Federals block lemons from getting to us). Momma, Sissy, and I and our boarders joined the parade and carried trays of what was to have been our Sunday dinner down to the station.

While we were carrying food and drink to the main streets and waiting for the wounded, we were in high spirits. Activity seemed to fuel our optimism. It was like a celebration for these mighty men, and the women chattered eagerly. But when the tattered, bloody, wounded soldiers began to arrive, many of them unable to walk to the food and drink we'd provided, the women and girls hushed in reverance. We went from soldier to soldier, who were lying on the edge of the streets waiting for someone to take them home to nurse them. We lifted groggy heads to give sips of lemonade and broke corn pones into small bites for those who could not feed themselves. More than once, I had to fight back tears as I thought about the mothers and sisters that wished they could cradle these boys' heads instead of me.

Those who were not as wounded in body were just as broken in spirit. These soldiers talked in hushed voices, not bragging about victories, but remembering the battle and their fallen comrades. They told us that the Confederacy had half as many soldiers as the Yankees in that battle. The air hung thick with the question I wondered if they were thinking and I knew was on most of our minds: How many more of these brave souls must both sides lose before it is over?

Tonight Charlie told me a man by the name of Timothy Webster was sentenced to death for spying for the Union. He used to take letters and packages from Richmond to Baltimore, including important information from the Confederate generals. When he got there, he'd open them, copy the important sections, and send the information on to Washington. Emma, do you think our letters are ever opened? What do we know of our mail courier? I know Great Auntie trusts him, but many people trusted Timothy Webster too.

Folks are shocked. No one suspected him at all. What will they think of Miss Van Lew now? They already suspect her of Union sympathies.

Your friend,

Mollie

Camp near Hampton, Virginia

APRIL 8, 1862

Dear Mollie,

Sorry for such a brief letter on the other side, but when you read this long letter in our secret ink, you will know my reason for caution. Chaplain B said he knew of a situation he could get for me if I had sufficient moral courage to undertake its duties. This morning, a detachment of the Thirty-Seventh New York rode out as scouts and brought back several Rebel prisoners. One of them reported that a Federal Secret Service agent, who was spying for the Union in the lands of the Confederacy, had been captured in Richmond. Chaplain B said the Union Army needs a replacement for this spy to get important battle plans and information to our generals. "However," he said, "it is a situation of great danger and vast responsibility. You know from your job as the regiment's mail carrier just how much danger there is. As a Secret Service agent, though, Frank, if you are caught, we cannot help you. You will be tried and hung for treason."

I rode off alone for a few hours to consider the task. Was I capable of performing the duties of a spy with honor and excellence? I certainly knew how to fool people with a disguise! I have been doing that now for several years, both with civilians and now in the army.

I ride hard and fast. I am quick and clever. I am observant and have a good memory.

And I do not worry for my life. I leave that in the hands of my Creator, feeling assured that I am just as safe passing through the picket lines of the enemy, if it is God's will that I should go there, as I would be in my tent in Federal camp. And if not, then his will be done.

I rode back to speak privately with Chaplain B. Yes, he could submit my name to headquarters as a willing volunteer for this duty.

Your friend,

Emma

Washington, D.C.

APRIL 10, 1862

Dear Mollie,

General McClellan, General Heinzelman, and General Meagher interviewed me at General McClellan's headquarters for the position in the Secret Service. I answered all their questions truthfully. They assumed, of course, I was who I appeared to be—Franklin Thompson, the private of Company F, Second Michigan Volunteer Infantry Regiment.

When they examined my ability with firearms. I passed with flying colors. (See, Mollie, I told you I can outshoot any soldier!) General Meagher remarked that my small size would likely help me to slip in and out of places others could not go. I told them I was sure I could disguise myself too, if needed. Finding me fit for the assignment, they administered the oath of allegiance to the Union, which I proudly affirmed. The generals complimented my faithful service to the Union so far, and Chaplain B could not have been prouder.

With such a short time to prepare for my debut as a spy, I may not be able to write for a while. I have to admit, Mollie, these new duties in the Secret Service of the United States government are exactly what I was meant to do. I can feel it. I'm sure to have some grand adventures. I hope I don't run out of our special ink so I can write you all about them!

Your friend,

Emma

Richmond, Virginia

APRIL 12, 1862

Dear Emma,

Miss Van Lew seemed quieter today on our way to Libby Prison. Of course, I chattered as usual. There are so few people I can have these discussions with. But, today, Miss Van Lew seemed a bit anxious. I wonder if it's because of Timothy Webster.

We left books and took back others, as usual. This time she didn't flip through them as was her custom, but simply loaded up both our baskets and hurried back to her home. When we arrived there, Nelson met her, wearing a worried look. They disappeared for a few minutes into the library.

When she returned, Miss Van Lew said I should leave. No biscuit. No milk. No new books. When I reminded her that I needed a new book to read, she pulled one from her basket and slipped it into mine. With apologies and excuses about not feeling well, she hurried me out the door.

I thought about it all the way home, Emma. Something is definitely up in that house. This seems to be a time for secrets. Your secret. The secrets of spies. Secret hiding places for Confederate valuables. The secrets I'm sure Miss Van Lew has hidden in that house.

Tonight we went to St. Paul's to sew bandages and sandbags to fortify the city. Does that mean the battle lines are drawn at our city gates? The ladies said that President Davis might send his family farther south. It certainly makes you wonder how close Richmond is to destruction.

Can our city stand up to an invasion? What would they do with us if they conquer our city? Do we go to prison too? I mean, if the President of the Confederacy is going to send his family away, is it wise to stay? Will our home be taken over by the enemy anyway? Should we try to join Great Auntie in Baltimore? My head hurts from trying to figure this out. It seems like we're all very busy right now preparing for the attack, but we're not busy enough to keep these thoughts from bombarding me. I don't dare voice them. I have no idea if Momma and Sissy are thinking the same thing. I don't want to be afraid, but if truth be told, Emma, I very much am.

Tonight, Momma had Sissy and me pull up the floorboards in the attic and hide our family silver. More secrets.

Your friend,

Mollie

Richmond, Virginia

April 21, 1862

Dear Emma,

Your last two letters finally reached me. Emma Edmonds! Just when I finished reading your letter about your shooting the pistol out of the hand of the Rebel stealing your horse, I turned to your letter reporting that you've agreed to become a spy! If you're found out, you could be hung for treason. It's one thing to help the Federal cause by nursing Federal wounded soldiers back to health. But now you will venture into Confederate lands and Rebel camps as a spy. It's too much to risk. Are you sure you weren't all puffed up with pride at the idea? Did you really think about the consequences? Sure I worried about you before—after all, they could discover that you're a girl. But what was the worst that could happen? You'd be kicked out of the army. What is the worst that can happen if they discover that you're a spy? Oh, Emma, I can't bear the thought. Please reconsider.

General Magruder marched thousands of his men through the streets of Richmond yesterday! From early in the morning until evening, the marchers continued through the city cheered on by the crowds, the drummers, and lively tunes played by the military bands. From every window, you could see smiling girls waving handkerchiefs and cheering on the men.

Great Auntie is concerned for us. She wants us to come to Baltimore to stay with her. Momma is frightened, I can tell, but refuses to leave the home she had with Daddy. I can understand that.

This afternoon, Momma asked me to take the silver candelabra up to the attic to find a suitable hiding place. Sissy and I had already worked up all the loose boards for the other silver we hid, so there didn't seem to be much hope in storing them underfoot. I looked around the attic and saw a bit of fabric poking out from behind a rafter in the roof. I stood on a few boxes on top of each

other, and pulled at the edge of the fabric behind the rafter. It wouldn't budge. I pulled harder, and to my great surprise, a packet of letters fluttered down from the rafter. They had been wrapped up in a handkerchief—one of Daddy's handkerchiefs!

My heart beat quickly as I gathered the letters. I put the handkerchief up to my face and felt its softness. I began to cry. I miss Daddy so terribly much. All of his women—Momma, Sissy, and me—have tried to be so brave during this unsettling time, but I know we all wish Daddy with his quiet strength was present with us now.

There were three letters. One addressed to Momma, one to Sissy, and one to me. I carefully placed Momma's and Sissy's letters on a box and sat down on the other box with Daddy's letter in my hand. Why had he written them? And why had they been hidden, in the rafters of the roof, where we were unlikely to ever find them?

I carefully opened his letter to me. It was written in 1859, six months before he died. I have copied it for you.

Dearest Mollie,

If you are reading this letter, then the great war I feared would come upon this country has begun. Perhaps you are in the attic hiding valuables. Perhaps even you, your sister, and your mother have had to hide in the attic. My guess is that you, Mollie, found these letters. You were always the most observant of us all. Ever since you were a young child, you watched and waited, observing, learning, calculating, taking it all in. Only then would you venture to act.

My dear Mollie, these are perilous times, and you have been placed in these times for a reason. I have been spared the pain of going through them. If you are reading this letter, then I am now safe with our Lord. Yet even now, I can see that troubles are upon us. This is why I am writing to you a special letter that is meant for your eyes alone.

I too am observant, Mollie, and I have seen how you have leaned into the thinking of the Greats, as you dearly love to call them. You know I was raised with their thinking as well, and as you've grown up

you probably heard me more times than not get into a heated discussion with your mother's relatives. I know you often wondered what I thought about slavery, abolition, and the views that divide our great country, but you were very young for me to discuss such things with you then. I imagine you are quite the beautiful, smart young woman now, and I want to share more of my thoughts with you.

Mollie, I cannot reconcile slavery with my beliefs in a loving God who would give the life of his Son for every man. Slavery states that a certain class of men, women, and children do not deserve freedom. To call someone a slave is to label that person as property, just as you would a wagon. But an enslaved person has a soul. An enslaved person has a heart beating in his breast for freedom. God designed all people that way—to love liberty and freedom. Otherwise, we would not recognize our own bondage to sin and our need for freedom in Christ.

If you are reading this letter, in the midst of a great war over the issue of slavery and other issues that divide the North from the South, I imagine you have wondered many times what I would have done if I had lived to see this day. From this vantage point, I cannot say much about what is going on in your life now. It has likely been years since these words were written. At least, I hope the conflict stays away that long. But, Mollie, if you find yourself wondering what your father would have done, ask yourself this — what would you do? What would you risk in this war for your beliefs?

Know that your father loves you more than he can bear. As I write this, I fight back the tears that threaten to wash away these words. I want to be healed, but if I am not, and I go to be with the Lord, know that I am proud of you and love you very much. As Uncle Chester says, "Mollie, you have a good head on those pretty shoulders of yours." Yes, Mollie, you have a good head and a good heart. Use them wisely. Pray often. The Lord will show you what to do.

With all my love,
Daddy

I let the letter fall to the floor and buried my head in my hands and sobbed. When all was spent inside me, I brushed the final tears from my face and lifted my apron to dry my eyes. I picked up the letter and read it again and again. Then I took the other two letters to Momma and Sissy. Emma, it was a sad and happy day in our home. We each slept with Daddy's letter to us tucked under our pillows that night.

Your friend,

Mollie

Richmond, Virginia

APRIL 30, 1862

Dear Emma,

They hanged Timothy Webster here yesterday for spying for the Union. Spying is dangerous business. I beg you to change your mind. Ask for a different assignment. I can't bear to think about losing you to such a horrid fate.

Throngs of families are leaving Richmond. The call for women to sew thousands of sandbags to fortify the city frightens me. It seems that is all we've been doing lately—sewing bandages and sandbags. What kind of invasion are they expecting anyway? Will thousands of you Federals pour into our city at any moment?

Great Auntie begged us to secure passes to visit her and leave Richmond too. There is a feeling of panic in the city as many pack up and leave. I admit I am terrified too as it seems as though soon the city will be a battlefield. Momma says we'll stay here no matter what. Momma keeps Daddy's letter with her at all times. I don't know what it said, but she is calmer now and stronger. Sissy is also determined to stay, that is until she learns where Lem's unit will be. With all we've heard about the advancing Northern troops, I think even she will stay put.

I haven't seen Miss Van Lew in several weeks. So much has been happening that I haven't had much time to read either. Last night, I pulled the book she gave me out of my basket. It was a medical book on fevers. I remembered how distracted Miss Van Lew was that day and realized she must have put the book in my basket by mistake. I decided to take it back to her.

As I put the book back in the basket, I noticed something strange about the spine. When I turned the book and held it up to the light, I saw a faint impression. Could there be something hidden in the spine of the book? I took a knife and very carefully pulled the leather of the spine away from the book. A small piece of paper fell

out. It was two inches by two inches with writing on it that made no sense to me at all. It looked like some kind of cipher or code. I copied it down on another sheet of paper. Then I put it back in the spine of the book and put the book in my basket.

I started out the door, but instead of turning left toward Miss Van Lew's, I turned right. I had to think. I kept walking, not really knowing where I might end up. What would I say to Miss Van Lew when I returned the book? Should I let her know that I found the coded message inside? Was it important? It's been there awhile, so surely any message it might contain for the Federals would be long out of date. Perhaps it is best, I reasoned, not to say anything at all.

I walked and walked for two hours. Finally, I realized I had come to the cemetery where Daddy was buried. I found his grave and sat down in the fresh spring grass. Like Momma, I keep Daddy's letter with me at all times. I pulled it out of my pocket and read it again. This time, something jumped out at me. Daddy had told me what he thought about slavery, and I agreed. But Daddy had not told me what he would do about it. Would he be like Constance and her family and still fight for the Confederacy even though they abhor slavery, or would he have found himself on the side of the Federals?

I realized it was not so important that I know what he would do. It was more important that I decide what I would do. And what would I do with this information I had found? Spy fever is very hot here in Richmond right now. Just take this book to the authorities, and Miss Van Lew would no longer be in business.

I jumped up, brushed off my skirt, and began the long walk to Miss Van Lew's home. When I got there, I found she had just gotten home from a visit to Libby Prison.

"Come in, Miss Mollie. I've been wondering when you would come for more books." She opened the door wide and ushered me into her parlor. "Would you care for some milk and biscuits?"

"Not today," I answered. "I came to return a book—a book I don't think you meant to give me."

Miss Van Lew looked at me quizzically and then glanced at the title of the volume I had placed in her hands. She quickly looked at me again. I remained stone-faced, though I saw her run her fingers along the spine. *She knows*, I thought.

"You brought this book back to me, Mollie. Why?"

"To return it, of course, and get another," I replied.

"This book is different," she said.

"Oh yes," I said with a laugh. "I think it's something my great uncle might like to read. He's a doctor, but I had no interest in a book on fevers, Miss Van Lew."

"Hmmm."

"My great uncle is a surgeon with the *Union* Army," I added.

Miss Van Lew looked at me in surprise. "Really?"

"Yes, he and my great aunt believe I have a good head on my shoulders."

"That you do. And what did you think of this book?"

"Oh, I didn't read it, Miss Van Lew. As soon as I touched it and read the title on the spine, I knew that this book was not meant for me."

"Hmm," said Miss Van Lew. She turned toward the window, hugging the book to her chest. After a few minutes, she twirled around, and said, "I think I have another book that you might like." She walked to the library and came back with a book on codes and ciphers used in previous wars. "Why don't you take this book and see if you find anything in it that interests you."

Curious, I took the book and placed it in my basket and bid her a good day. There was much we had said to one another, and much we had left unsaid. We were playing a cat and mouse game. I wanted to see if she was a spy. She wanted to see if I could be trusted.

I went home that night and read through the book on ciphers and codes, alongside the coded message I had copied. I'm good in mathematics, but I found it hard going. After midnight, I gave up and turned down my light.

Your friend,

Mollie

Richmond, Virginia

MAY 5, 1862

Dear Emma,

I've been hard at work for days now trying to crack this coded message. I can't do it. I'm convinced Miss Van Lew has a special cipher for the message—maybe it's one she made up herself. I've decided I won't turn her in. Somehow I have to make her understand that.

I took one of the more simple codes I found in the book and created my own secret message. This is what it said: "You can trust me. I want to help." When I put it in code, it read: WGS ACL RTSUR KG G UCLV RQ FGJR. I folded the small slip of paper, carefully slit open the spine of the book, and tucked the message inside. If she is a spy, she'll look there, and she'll know how to unscramble my message.

Once again, I was off to Grace Street with a book in my basket. I knocked on the door and Miss Van Lew answered the door. "Mollie!" she exclaimed. "Back so soon? The book was that easy to read?"

I came in and said, "Oh, no. I found it fascinating, but I imagine that all the codes one might have for a secret message are not contained in this book."

"Probably not," she agreed. I saw her finger the spine, almost unconsciously, when I gave her the book. She put it down on the table by us and said, "Mollie Turner, there comes a time in everyone's life when they must determine what risks they're willing to take for what they believe. Josiah Henson did that when he ran away with his family. They could have been captured. Imprisoned. Even killed."

Somehow I knew she wasn't talking about runaway slaves. I think she was trying to tell me about herself. She was so cryptic though. I had to think hard to stay with her as she continued to talk.

"And like Mr. Henson, he was never sure who he could trust. Who might he depend on to help him with his plans to get his slave family to freedom forever? At points of great necessity, like when he needed food for his family or passage across the river, he revealed who he was or what his purposes were. Sometimes, he had to judge the character of a man or a woman ... or a girl ... to determine who could be trusted. Sometimes, by depending on a few good-hearted souls, he was able to secure his highest hopes. Life is like that."

All right, I said to myself. She's talking about us. She wants to know if she can trust me. More cat and mouse games. She's wondering if her judgment of my character is accurate. I understand. One false move and her whole enterprise will come crashing down. Just look at Mr. Webster. He got away with spying for the Union for a long time, but then one person revealed his secret.

I stood to leave. "Thanks for the book, but I think there's much more you could teach me than what's contained in that book." And then I left.

I understand her caution, but now that I'm ready, I wish she would trust me. Emma, I want to help the Union any way I can. I don't think this friendship with Miss Van Lew came by accident.

Your friend,

Mollie

Richmond, Virginia

MAY 10, 1862

Dear Emma,

Our courier delivered your letters and he also had a package for me. It was wrapped in brown paper and tied with string. I thought it was from Great Auntie until I opened it. It was the same old book on codes and ciphers.

I took it to my room and looked for the slit in the spine. There I found a small piece of paper with a coded message. It looked to be the same code I used before. I unscrambled the words and read: "Come to Grace Street. I do trust you."

I quickly gathered my basket and put the spine of the book back together. When I got to Miss Van Lew's house, she greeted me with a plate of biscuits and butter and a glass of cool buttermilk. But I was too excited to eat.

"I pondered it for many nights. You could have turned me in. Instead, you returned my book with the message safe inside. You are a clever girl, and you found a simple way to let me know that you knew I was passing on messages from the Federal prisoners at Libby Prison to the Federal government. You also found a way to let me know you want to help.

"Are you sure, Mollie? Are you sure you want to get involved in this? I know I'm watched. I'm sure they have seen your comings and goings here as well."

I told her that I wanted to do all I could to bring this war to an end as quickly as possible and to bring this country — a country where all people can be free—back together again.

"Mollie, I'm not sure it will be that easy," she replied, "but every person has a role to play in this great conflict. I cannot sit idly by. I sensed from the moment that I met you that you could not either. Are you ready for your first assignment?"

I nodded yes.

"The code I use is not one in these books. You were smart enough to figure that out. I will not give you the cipher to it either. We will make up a special code just for the two of us to use. Sometimes you'll carry messages that you'll not be able to decipher. That is best for your safety."

"How will that work exactly?" I asked.

"Just like today," she continued, "the courier will bring you a book." When my eyes widened with disbelief, she added, "Yes, the man your great aunt selected is part of our group. He can be trusted. Check the spine of the book for the messages. Your job will be to get it to the next relay station. I am constantly watched. You'll be a big help."

"Who is the next person I take the message to?" I asked.

"There will be two coded messages in the spine of the book. One will be the message you are to carry. The other will be our own code, one that only the two of us have the cipher for. That is where you will get the information for the person who is to take the message next." We sat there for another hour, working out our own code and cipher. I can tell no one, not even you, dear Emma. But I'm sure you understand.

Before I left, Miss Van Lew explained that I might notice her beginning to act a bit strangely. "The folks in Richmond already think I'm off my rocker because of my Union views. Why not take it a bit further and let them think I've gone completely crazy? Don't be surprised by what you see me do or say. But, it won't do for you to come by the house anymore. My demise into insanity should be a good cover for your staying away. The books will come to you like today by the trusted mail courier, so it's just as likely they came to you from your great aunt."

"But I so enjoy our talks and our times together. I don't want them to end. I've learned so much from you."

"Oh, child, they are not over. They're just postponed for a bit. We will have times like this again. The Union must survive, and when it does, we can talk again. Until then, it's much safer for you to stay away. Besides, once you see Old Crazy Bet, your mother will not want you here again!"

We laughed and I hugged her good-bye. This time, I only left with a biscuit in my basket.

Your friend,

Mollie

Near Williamsburg, Virginia

MAY 15, 1862

Dear Mollie,

I purchased a suit of clothing, plantation style, at Fortress Monroe for my first disguise, so I would appear to be a hard working slave. Then I had the barber shave my hair close to my head. I colored my head, face, neck, hands, and arms dark with silver nitrate and put on a wig of black hair. I tried out my disguise on James. I told him my name was Ned, a fugitive slave, and offered to clean his boots. When I returned them, he thanked me and gave me some money. He didn't recognize Frank at all!

I put a few hard crackers in my pocket and with my revolver loaded and capped, I started out on foot at dusk without a blanket or anything that might create suspicion. About nine-thirty that night, I passed through the outer picket line of the Union Army. By midnight, I crept past a sentinel and got within the Rebel lines. I went on a safe distance from the picket lines and lay down and rested until morning. Notice that I said I rested. I surely didn't sleep. My heart was pounding too loudly. I've met enough fugitive slaves to know what the Rebels do to runaways when they are caught. This disguise might help me once I'm in the camp and working with the other slaves, but until then, I'm nothing but a runaway to be captured, whipped—or worse.

Early the next morning before dawn, I made my way to the Rebel camp. I met a group of slaves carrying coffee and food to the Rebel pickets. They gave me a cup of coffee and a piece of corn bread. The slaves reported to work on the Rebel fortifications. I followed and watched them as they worked. One of the officers came up to me and said, "Whose are you, and why are you not at work?"

"Name's Ned. I'm free and goin' to Richmond to get some work."

The officer shoved me and said to the foreman, "Take that rascal and set him to work. If he don't work well, tie him up and give him

twenty lashes. That'll teach him that there's no such thing as free slaves here!"

I joined about a hundred other slaves who were building the fort. I took a pickaxe, shovel, and wheelbarrow and did whatever my companions in bondage did. The portion of the parapet that I was building was eight feet high. With the help of another slave, I wheeled gravel in the wheelbarrows to the top of the parapet. I worked until my hands were blistered and raw. But, as I worked, I kept my eyes and ears open.

When night came, they let us roam around the fortifications. Then I made a sketch of the outer works of the fort and a list of all the guns I saw that night. I put both papers in the inner sole of my shoe and returned to the slave quarters. I knew I could not shovel or carry wheelbarrows the next day with my blistered hands. I found a lad about my own size who had been carrying water, and paid him to swap places with me for the next few days.

The second day was much easier. During my water carrying duties, I learned the number of reinforcements that arrived from different places and even saw General Robert E. Lee. I carried water to my slave friends. One of them looked at me strangely and said, "Jim, I think that fella is turning white!" My heart raced, but I made a joke, and they laughed at me. I got off by myself as soon as I could to take out my small pocket looking glass. Sure enough, I was getting lighter. I took my small vial of silver nitrate and applied some more of it to prevent the remaining color from coming off.

On the third day as I filled the soldiers' canteens, I heard a familiar voice. It was the peddler who used to come to our Federal camp and headquarters weekly with newspapers and stationery. Now, here he was with the Rebels, giving them a full description of our camp and forces! He also brought out a map of the entire placement of General McClellan's positions! That traitor! I had to get back with this information!

That night I slipped noiselessly through the woods to the picket line. I gave the familiar signal to our pickets, and they let me

through the Federal lines. I went straight to General McClellan's headquarters, presented my report, and received the hearty congratulations of the general himself!

It was a great day. My slave costume was put away for another day and my Frank costume was put back on. Only you know me as Emma. I'm glad someone knows my true self.

I had to postpone my second visit into enemy territory. On May 5, General Hooker attacked the Rebels near Williamsburg, and the Second Michigan was ordered there as reinforcements. We marched eight miles in the drenching rain. By the fifth mile, I could no longer feel my toes. The shoe leather on my boots isn't that great. The holes in my boots made them fill with water which only blistered my feet faster. I wasn't sure if I could make it, but James marched beside me, encouraging me on. When we got to the battlefield, some of our company joined the fight, and the rest of us set up the field hospitals.

The fighting was fierce and many of our own were wounded. I worked for days with the surgeons. I've learned to try to push out any thoughts about the wounded soldier's body and concentrate more on his soul. If I focus on the wounds, which are often so massive, I lose heart and can't do my job. So many of these brave men are so young. After the battle, James helped me, and we moved as many as we could to the churches and college buildings in Williamsburg.

Time after time, a soldier who knew he was dying would ask for the chaplain. If none was there, I would send James. He'd wipe their brow and listen as a soldier would whisper his last words. So often, the message was the same: "Tell Mother that Christ does not desert the dying soul." "Tell Mother I died believing in Jesus." That's our only comfort, isn't it, in perilous times like these — that because of Jesus, we will see each other again one day?

Your friend,

Emma

Richmond, Virginia

May 22, 1862

Dear Emma,

It was not long before the first book arrived. It came just like Miss Van Lew said it would, wrapped in brown paper and tied with string. The courier gave it to me with letters from you and Great Auntie.

I took the package to my room and opened it. Inside the spine of the book, I found the coded messages. One I could not decipher. I laid the other side by side with my code and unscrambled the message. It gave me the name of a clerk in a store a few blocks away and the code word "peaches." I assumed he was part of Miss Van Lew's relay network to get messages through to the Federal lines.

A few hours later, I left the house with the coded message folded up in a hollowed out acorn with the top securely back on. This tiny acorn couldn't possibly be seen in my pocket, but I was so afraid, I thought everyone I passed knew what I was carrying. When I got to the store, I asked Mr. Simpson if he had any peaches. He looked up, surprised. My heart started beating quickly. Of course, this isn't peach season. Maybe I'd unscrambled the message wrong. My face flushed hot, and my heart pounded in my chest.

"I think I have a jar back here, young lady. Follow me." When we got to the back of the store, I took the acorn out of my pocket and started to hand it to him. He pointed to a peach pit pin on his watch chain and turned away. Miss Van Lew warned me about this. The peach pit was carved like a clover. If my contact held the clover down, then it was safe to talk. If he held it up, we were to go our separate ways. He held it up. It wasn't safe to talk. My eyes darted around the store. A man watched us over his newspaper. My right hand gripped the acorn in my pocket so tightly that I thought it might shatter. I pushed the acorn deeper in my pocket, turned on my heels, and called out, "Oh well, I guess I'll try another day. Momma did so want a taste of pickled peaches for her supper tonight."

When I got outside, I practically ran down the block. I was so frightened that I gasped for air. What should I do? Now I had a message that needed to be delivered and my contact told me I couldn't leave it. How would I know when I could come back?

I walked a few more blocks and then turned back for home. When I got within a block of the store again, a kindly old man walked up to me with a flower. "A pretty flower for a pretty girl with a good head on her shoulders?" I gave a start. Was this a secret message? How odd! I took the flower and stared at the old man. But he just passed on and gave another flower to the next girl saying the same thing.

I kept jiggling the acorn in my pocket. This was simply not going to work. I made my way back home and sat on the veranda puzzled and confused. It was a hot day. How I longed for lemonade. One day, when this cruel war is over, I'll drink gallons and gallons of lemonade—with lots of sugar. I couldn't stand sitting any longer. I walked to the edge of our lawn and looked for Charlie. Surely he would be coming down the sidewalk soon with his newspaper. A lady walked by and said, "You look miserably hot, my dear. Please take my fan." I protested, but she insisted, and handed me her straw palm fan, and walked on down the street.

I sat back down on the verandah and fanned myself over and over. It did feel good. Suddenly, I sat up straight in the rocking chair. The fan had writing on it: *Capitol Square.*

This spying business is exhausting. I jumped up and practically ran to Capitol Square. It was crowded today with lots of women and girls admiring the flowers. The fan came in handy since it was quite warm. It seemed strange to me that I should bring my secret message right here to the grounds of the Confederate government. A lovely woman that I hadn't seen before in Richmond approached me. "It's a gorgeous day, isn't it?"

I was quite wary of her. "Yes, lovely." I continued to fan myself with the fan.

"It's hard to believe fall will be right around the corner. Nothing like a gorgeous fall day with the tall oaks dropping their little acorns all around. You see that oak there? It's my favorite one."

I couldn't tell if this was a message or not. It sure was strange. I watched until she walked away. Then I thought I'd try an experiment. I walked over to the tree and slipped the acorn down between two roots of the tree. I walked away casually but stood near enough to watch. Sure enough, several minutes later, the lady came back and sat down under the tree pretending to read a book. But I saw her gently pick up the acorn and put it in her pocket. After fifteen minutes, she stood up to leave.

This spy business is complicated. When I got home, Momma said I had a message from the store that my pickled peaches were in. What! Had I just left the acorn message with the wrong person? I thanked Momma, who looked very puzzled. Momma asked me why I thought we could afford pickled peaches right now, and why I was going to this store, which was not our usual shop. I had to do some quick thinking. I didn't want to lie to Momma, but I couldn't tell her everything. Finally, I gambled and said, "Miss Van Lew told me to go there for these peaches. She has some on her farm outside of the city, so these won't cost us a penny." That seemed to satisfy Momma. I could tell she wished she could have a bite of those peaches soon.

I ran down to the store. Mr. Simpson had his peach pit pin turned the other way. He gave me a jar of pickled peaches to take home and said he wanted me to know the secret message was safely on its way. It turns out the lady who gave me the fan is his wife, Mrs. Simpson. The lady I met in the park, the one who took the acorn, is his daughter. They all help with taking the messages to the next station.

I'll be happy if it's weeks before I have another message to send on up the lines!

Your friend,

Near the Chickahominy River

MAY 23, 1862

Dear Mollie,

We camped along the Chickahominy River waiting for the men to finish the bridges across the river. Staying near the river made me long for home. How often I fished in those rivers in New Brunswick. We'd cook fish right out of those rivers with taters for breakfast. Now all I get to do in the rivers is ride through them or march over them.

I got my second assignment to see what I could learn about the enemy's troops and weapons. After the battle in Williamsburg earlier in the month, I bought a dress of an Irish peddler woman. Imagine that now— Emma the girl, disguised as Frank the boy, disguised as Bridget, the Irish peddler woman.

I packed my disguise in a pie basket and swam my horse across the river. Then I gave him a farewell pat and let him swim back again to the other side, where a soldier waited for his return. It was now evening. I didn't know the exact distance to the picket line, but I thought it best to avoid the roads. I slept near the swamp that night.

It took me some time to get my disguise right. I put on the river-soaked dress and hid my uniform in the woods. The food I had carefully packed in the basket was wet and rotting. I certainly looked like a broken-hearted forlorn Bridget who should never have left Ireland. After several hours traveling in the swamp, and trying out my Irish brogue on the birds and the squirrels, I saw a small white house in the distance.

I thought it was deserted, but when I came inside, I saw a sick Rebel soldier, lying on a straw mattress on the floor. Assuming my Irish brogue, I asked him if I could help. Barely alive from the last skirmish with the Federals, he spoke in a whisper. He had crawled on his hands and knees to take refuge in this deserted house, but he thought he had typhoid.

I was just inside the door and had not moved any closer. Typhoid. I was already soaked and chilled from the night air of the river. What if I were to catch typhoid? That would be the end of Frank, and the end of my spying days. I'd already had one close call with my fever in Washington. I would never survive being found out if I had typhoid. Standard treatment was to daily give a typhoid patient a cool bath.

The sick soldier slipped back into deep sleep. I couldn't decide what to do. Everything in me said to turn and get out of there before I caught typhoid too. He was so unaware that he'd never know I'd been there. I looked at his pale face and decided I would leave, but first I'd warm a fire and make him some food to leave within reach.

I kindled a fire, found some flour and corn meal, and baked a large hoe cake. I heated some water for tea. To my surprise, the soldier rallied and spoke quietly. He was a Confederate soldier, but I saw no hatred of the Yankees in him. I asked if he was a soldier of the cross. He replied. "Yes, thank God! I have fought longer under the Captain of my salvation than I have under Jeff Davis."

I knew I had to stay then. I couldn't let this man die alone. I fed the poor famished Rebel as tenderly as if he'd been my own brother. He thanked me with as much politeness as if I'd been Mrs. Jefferson Davis. I longed to restore him to health and strength, not considering that the very health and strength I wished to secure for him would be used against the Union.

While he still had strength to answer, I had to know something. How could he fight for slavery if he called himself a disciple of Christ? I asked him gently and waited for his reply.

His face fell. "Oh, Bridget, you have touched a point upon which my own heart condemns me." We talked a bit more, but he was failing fast.

I found a little bit of salt pork and corn meal and made gruel for my patient, but he barely swallowed it. "Dear Bridget, tell me true, am I dying?"

"Yes, my new friend, you are dying. Have you made your peace with God?"

He sighed and then whispered, "My trust is in Christ. He was mine in life, and in death he will not forsake me." I leaned close, and he asked me to find the Confederate camp between here and Richmond and let Major McKee of General Ewell's staff know what had happened to him.

No longer fearing for my own safety, I held him until he struggled in his breathing. He gained some strength and whispered, "Glory to God. I am almost home!" He labored a few hours more, and then, in my arms, he slipped away to heaven. I thank God, Mollie. It was my privilege to be there. I know God led me to that deserted house so he would not die alone. If I get typhoid as a result and am found out or die, I do not regret this decision.

The next morning, I found a number of articles in the cabin that helped me perfect my disguise: mustard, pepper, an old pair of spectacles, and a bottle of red ink. With the mustard powder, I made a strong plaster and tied it on my face until it blistered thoroughly. I then covered my blistered face with court plaster. With ink, I painted a red line around my eyes, as if I'd been crying. I put on the green glasses and my Irish hood, which covered about six inches of my face. I filled my baskets with other items in the house that an Irish peddler woman might be expected to have. Then I buried my pistol and anything else that might create suspicion.

After I had walked five miles, I saw the Rebel sentinel ahead. I sat down to rest and steady myself for this interview. I took the black pepper from my basket and sprinkled some of it on my handkerchief, and applied it to my eyes to start the tears running down my face. Looking in the mirror, I saw a sad, sad lady indeed. When I met the guard, I told him my sorrowful story of running away from the Yankees. I lifted my peppery handkerchief to my eyes until tears ran down my face in steady streams. With my best Irish brogue, I sobbed my miserable story, and the guard let me pass on my way to the Rebel camp.

Once at the camp, I easily overheard news of the enemy's troops — both their position and their strength. Everyone was talking about the upcoming battle. I had plenty of information and needed to get back to the river, but I had a duty to perform for a brother in Christ, even if he was an enemy in this war.

I went to the headquarters and asked for Major McKee. In my best Irish brogue, I told him the story and delivered the soldier's watch and his letters. I didn't need the black pepper to help me cry as I thought about this man.

Major McKee rose to his feet and said, "You are a faithful woman, and you shall be rewarded. Can you direct the men to that house to show them where Captain Hall's body is?" When I nodded yes, he gave me a ten-dollar greenback, saying as he did so, "If you succeed in finding the house, I'll give you more."

I thanked him but wouldn't take the money. He looked at me suspiciously, for why would a poor old beggar woman not take whatever money she could get? I was scared, Mollie. I thought I might have blown my cover. Suddenly, I burst into a passionate fit of weeping. "Oh General, forgive me. My conscience would never let me take money for carrying a message that the boy is dead. Oh, my, I could never do such a terrible thing." He seemed satisfied, and when he returned with his men, I begged him for a horse to ride, saying that I had been sick for several days.

I rode at the head of the band of Rebels as a guide. The Rebels wished they had brought an ambulance, but I thought this better suited my plan. The men went into the house and brought out Captain Hall's body on a stretcher. The sergeant asked me to ride down the road a little way and if I saw any Yankees to ride back as fast as possible and let them know. I happily complied with the first part of his request. I rode down the road slowly, and not seeing or hearing anything of the Yankees, thought it best to keep going until I did!

I rode steadily on until I reached the Chickahominy, where I reported what I had learned of the Rebel troop movements to the general. I said nothing of the band of men carrying Captain Hall's body back to camp. Then I talked with James at the campfire for hours. It was hard not to say anything to him about these missions. I've shared so much with him in this war, but this duty I can't share with any of my comrades. Keeping secrets from one's good friend is a price I will pay willingly if it will advance the cause of the Union.

Just got word—we've been ordered out tomorrow for battle. Pray for me, Mollie, as I pray for you.

Your friend,

Emma

Richmond, Virginia

JUNE 1, 1862

Dear Emma,

We hear the sounds of cannons here in Richmond. For weeks now, wagons heaped with trunks, boxes, and baskets have constantly rattled through the streets as families flee Richmond. It certainly does not breed confidence in the Confederacy to see the new congressmen and their families leaving town like scared rabbits. It doesn't help either to see the boxes and boxes of government documents marked for Columbia, South Carolina, stacked high outside of government offices. Momma, Sissy, and I stay resolute. We will not leave our home. We went to St. Paul's the other day to sew ticking for beds for the wounded that are expected soon.

Last week, Mayor Mayo formed a Home Guard of boys 16 – 18 and men over 45. Charlie, almost fifteen, daily begs his mother to let him join the Confederates. She holds firm that he must be sixteen, but she told Charlie that if the Home Guard would let him enroll, she would permit it. Charlie was ecstatic. He was sure he could pass for a sixteen-year-old. Sure enough, Emma, he's now an official member of the Richmond Home Guard. He's determined to protect our dear city and marches around with a rusty musket gun that he doesn't know how to shoot.

What terrible news we hear! Losses are great on both sides. All this on the Sabbath, Emma. Oh, I do pray you are well.

Your devoted friend,

Mollie

Richmond, Virginia

June 3, 1862

Dear Emma,

If only I had word of your safekeeping. Sissy waits for word of Lem. Sunday night the steady trail of wagons, carts, ambulances, and trains brought the wounded into Richmond. Monday, hospitals and private homes were once again filled with broken and wounded men. Momma took in three boys to nurse with the help of our boarders. Sissy and I walked around the city for two days trying to get word on Lem.

We found Constance and Hetty searching for their cousin, Reggie Hyde, who they had heard was wounded. We walked down Main Street together, going in and out of churches, hotels, and hospitals looking for Reggie and Lem.

Everywhere we looked, we saw men desperately wounded and waiting for surgeons. Lying on bare boards, with only a knapsack under their heads, all were suffering horribly. Although we walked around the city all day, we didn't find Reggie or Lem. That night, Sissy and I fell exhausted onto our beds in our clothes.

When we checked the Ballard House Hotel, we didn't find our boys, but we did find newspaper reporters and plenty of curious citizens. Mrs. Greenhow and her five-year-old daughter had just arrived there. Mrs. Greenhow is the famous Confederate spy whom the Federals imprisoned with her daughter in the Capitol Prison in Washington. President Lincoln's Secretary of War just freed her. He permitted them to take a flag-of-truce boat to Richmond. I suppose he thinks her harmless now that she is among the Confederates. Strange. I'd think a lady this clever could do just as much damage to the Federal cause here in Richmond as she did in Washington.

So many spies, here, Emma. Famous spies. And some not so famous spies too!

Your friend,

Mollie

Richmond, Virginia

JUNE 7, 1862

Dear Emma,

The fighting of this last week has brought such sorrow to Richmond. Every day, more and more ambulances arrive in Richmond with broken soldiers. Sissy finally found Lem in a private hospital, bloody and suffering from a concussion. Thankfully, he still has all his arms and legs. Sissy brought him home to our house to nurse him. He is expected to make a full recovery.

I will never forget the sights of the battles. Constance and I watched the battles from the top of a building. Your spy balloons hovered over the field. Even at night, we saw the bursts of the bombs and the flash of thousands of muskets. The fighting is so close now. Constance and I threw our arms around each other for comfort. Although the fighting is staying outside the city, we know it may soon take place on our very streets. I was glad Constance was with me. Those Cary cousins seem to have more courage that I can muster. Each night, when we go to the top of the building, I wonder, is this the night I will actually hear the battles? When that happens, I will know the war is soon to overtake us.

In the midst of it all, I received another delivery! Another book in a plain brown wrapper tied up with string. I slit open the binding of the book and found another set of coded notes. Using my code, I found this message: *Roll of bandages. Same store.*

I took a roll of bandages and unrolled it. At the center I placed the coded message, and then rolled it back up again. The next morning, I went to Mr. Simpson's store. His wife was the proprietor that morning. I noticed she wore the peach pit pin. The clover design was pointing up so I knew not to speak with her about the message. "Do you have any more cloth for bandages, Mrs. Simpson?" I asked. "I can leave this roll with you, but I want to roll some more."

"I'm sorry, dear, we have no flannel or cotton right now," she

replied. "I'll make sure this roll of bandages gets to where it can best help this war. Thank you, dear!"

I slipped out of the store. This time, Emma, I felt a bit more confident. As I turned down the street, guess who I ran into—Miss Van Lew. Only, it didn't look like her at all. She was dressed in buckskin leggings, a torn skirt, a cotton shirt, and an oversized floppy calico bonnet. She appeared not to notice me, and sang little songs to herself. "Miss Van Lew!" I exclaimed. She walked right past me singing and talking to herself. I suppose this is the beginning of her Crazy Bet plan.

I walked behind her a bit just to study her outfit and ways. She kept humming and singing. As I turned around and walked away, I could see several of the women shaking their heads in disapproval of old Crazy Bet.

Your friend,

Mollie

Camp, near Richmond, Virginia

JUNE 10, 1862

Dear Mollie,

I am well, but the Battle of Fair Oaks marks me forever! At the beginning of the battle on May 31, General Kearny assigned me to be his acting orderly. I usually don't ride into battle. All day long, I rode wherever General Kearny rode and did whatever he asked me to do. You should see General Kearny in battle. The loss of his left arm from the Mexican War doesn't stop him one bit. Why, he catches his reins in his teeth and fights with his sword in his right hand!

The fighting was desperate. The rain-swollen Chickahominy River swamped the bridges and trapped the soldiers on the other side. General Kearny rode up and down the lines trying to encourage the men. He had sent several messages already to General McClellan at headquarters on the other side of the river about the need for reinforcements, but hours had gone by and none had arrived. Finally about two o'clock in the afternoon, General Kearny reined in his horse abruptly, took an envelope from his pocket, and wrote on the back of it: "In the name of God, bring your command to our relief, if you have to swim in order to get here—unless you come, we are lost." He handed it to me and said, "Go as fast as that horse can carry you to General Sumner, present this with my compliments, and return immediately to report to me."

I turned my horse and pushed him at top speed toward the river until he was nearly white with foam, then I plunged him into the Chickahominy River and swam him across. I met General Sumner about a hundred yards from the river. Engineers were working to strengthen the bridge, and General McClellan ordered General Sumner to cross as soon as he could to come to our aid. The soldiers began to pour across the river on the planks. The entire division made it to the other side and started down the flooded road double-time.

I swam my horse back across the river and raced to General

Kearney in the thickets of the fight. Riding up to him, I touched my hat and reported, "Just returned, sir. General Sumner, with his command, will be here immediately."

General Kearny swung around and shouted at the top of his voice, "Reinforcements! Reinforcements!" And swinging his hat in the air, he electrified the entire exhausted line.

Later that day, while I was riding with General Kearney, a minnie ball whizzed by me and struck General Howard, knocking him from his horse and shattering his arm. Securing permission from General Kearney to attend to him, I jumped down from my horse and hitched him nearby. I removed the cloth from General Howard's arm, gave him some water, poured some on the wound, and went to my saddlebags to get some bandages. Just then old Reb, the horse I took from the enemy during my second spying mission as Bridget, turned on me and bit me hard, tearing part of the flesh from my arm. Searing pain shot through my arm, but I made a sling and continued to help General Howard.

Later, after the battle, General Howard's arm was amputated above the elbow. General Kearney stayed with him the entire time. There are many wounded. We spent most of our days after the battle pouring cool water on the wounds while soldiers waited for the surgeons to tend to them. James suffered a flesh wound on his arm from a sword. I wrapped it in bandages and he is resting comfortably. My own arm is burning with pain. I won't let anyone else tend to it though. I insist that I can keep it wrapped. The surgeon lifted his eyebrow at my insistence. I quickly moved on to help another of the wounded, despite my pain, to reduce his suspicion. But tonight, I wish for more cool water to cool my burning arm.

The day after the battle, General Kearney presented me with a Confederate officer's sword which had been found on the battlefield. He said it was in appreciation for the great bravery I showed on the field as his orderly that day. In return, I gave him Reb, but warned him he should be kept away from any valiant officers he valued!

My arm hurts something awful, Mollie, but it will not need to be amputated. Don't worry, I can still write. I'm more discouraged of heart, though, as I reflect upon all I have seen during the Battle of Fair Oaks. We had our bravest generals with us, but still it didn't turn the tide.

Your friend,

Emma

Richmond, Virginia

JUNE 15, 1862

Dear Emma,

Charlie came by today bursting with news. General Jeb Stuart rode into town to meet with General Robert E. Lee. Emma, it isn't good news for the Federals. General Stuart and twelve hundred cavalrymen rode in a large circle around General McClellan's forces over the last four days to spy out how many men you have, how strong the forces are, and what positions you are in. He rode into town jauntily today with all his cavalry and more than a hundred Yankee prisoners, some runaway slaves, and some horses and mules behind him.

Richmond rejoices at this news! It was a bold move on the part of General Stuart. Sissy is ecstatic as Lem was one of those cavalrymen. I am sure General Lee will use this to his advantage. Please be careful.

Your friend,

Mollie

Richmond, Virginia

JUNE 16, 1862

Dear Emma,

Another mission today! As usual, I carved from the spine of the book the coded messages — one for another's eyes, one for mine. This time the message said: *Meet me. Libby.*

I couldn't tell from Miss Van Lew's message whether I was supposed to bring the coded message with me or not. I took a thick ribbon and wrapped it over the message several times and then tied it up in my hair. I walked quickly to the bench near Libby Prison and waited for Miss Van Lew. Crazy Bet showed up carrying a platter wrapped in a towel and a basket of books over her arm.

"Miss Van Lew," I said, "I thought we weren't going to be seen together again."

"Yes, I know, but much is happening now with General McClellan and his troops ready to enter Richmond. Time is of the essence, and I had to take this chance. New Federal prisoners arrived yesterday. I must get into the prison, and I need your help. More and more each day I arouse suspicion. I thought today a distraction in the way of a lovely young Rebel girl accompanying me might be nice."

"What's in the platter?"

"Nothing secretive this time," she replied. I knew Miss Van Lew had a platter with a false bottom that concealed letters and other information. "Just a wonderful custard. But I need a splendid conversationalist to keep them busy so that I can have as much time as possible inside the prison."

I thought for a few moments and then agreed to do it. "But what about the book you sent me ... and its message inside?"

"Yes. You can take that to Mrs. Simpson at the store. Later. Do you think you can give me at least twenty minutes inside?"

"Miss Van Lew, I think it will take them twenty minutes just to stop looking at you. You do look a sight!" Again we laughed, as she

looked down at her buckskin leggings, her calico skirt, her tattered shirt, and her floppy bonnet.

"Why, thank you, Miss Mollie! I get so many compliments on my new outfit."

We laughed again. "I bet you do!"

"The crazier they think I am," she explained, "the more they leave me alone."

My heart was pounding when we got inside. The warden nudged another guard and whispered, "Crazy Bet's here again."

"Kind sir, I came to collect my books. Miss Turner here will help me carry them back to my home. She is kind to me, although her mother doesn't like her associating with me much anymore." Then Miss Van Lew lowered her voice and whispered, "She thinks I'm crazy."

"I remember this young girl from your earlier trips to Libby, Miss Van Lew. She used to help you then—carry the books, I mean."

"Yes, and I prevailed on her one more time because of my heavy load. She is a dear. Nurses at Robertson Hospital most days."

At the sound of the beloved Confederate hospital run by Captain Sally Tompkins, the men seemed to relax. When Miss Van Lew explained the custard was for them to eat, they seemed more than willing to let her into the prison to visit the men. When she was gone, I offered to serve the warden and his officer some custard. They gathered plates, and I slowly dished out the sweet dessert.

"Do you know Captain Tompkins?" I asked.

"No, no we don't. But there isn't a wounded soldier who doesn't want to be assigned to her hospital," they responded. "Nearly all her charges live to see another battle."

"She's a remarkable woman," I continued, "and runs the hospital as well as any general."

As the men settled back in their chairs and began to enjoy their custard, I told them story after story of Captain Tompkins and Robertson Hospital. "The ladies of Richmond say it's their favorite hospital for volunteering. I don't know how much the men like it though. One day, I overheard a young man respond to one of the volunteers who asked if she could wash his face, 'Why ma'am, of course you can, but you'd be the fourteenth lady today to scrub it clean.'"

The men laughed, and I began to relax. I continued on with stories about Captain Sally, sewing at St. Paul's, Sissy's trips to follow Lem's regiment, and the number of wounded we have nursed in our home. By the time Miss Van Lew returned, they were thoroughly convinced of my Confederate sympathies.

I hoped it served to allay some suspicion about Miss Van Lew. But when she came back through again with the prison official, she was acting as crazy as ever. I leaned over to the warden and whispered, "We must do what we can for the less fortunate of the Richmond ladies, don't you agree? This war has affected her so." He nodded knowingly, and we slipped quickly out of the prison.

We hurried up the hill from the prison to Grace Street. I'd heard that Confederate General Johnson had been wounded at the Battle of Fair Oaks and was recuperating at his friend's house on Grace Street. Miss Van Lew confirmed it. Imagine that! Confederate generals and Federal spies on the same street!

I carried the platter into Miss Van Lew's house. As she served us cups of contraband tea her Federal contacts had given her, I mimicked Crazy Bet talking to the guards. Miss Van Lew laughed and said, "I hope that will throw them off for a while. Hopefully, it won't be much longer before General McClellan arrives and this is a Federal city again. Mother has made up a special guest room for the general. With what I learned today, it shouldn't be long. Now, Mollie, I want to add something to the message you already have. Would you be so kind as to wait while I encode the message?"

When she returned, I unwound my hair and ribbon, added the second message, and then wound it all up again. Miss Van Lew studied me solemnly the entire time. When it was time to leave, she gave me a hug and said, "From now on, when you see Crazy Bet, pay no attention to her. Remember your mother would not want you associating with the likes of Crazy Bet."

Your friend,

Mollie

Vicinity of Fair Oaks

June 27, 1862

Dear Mollie,

I needed to give my arm time to heal from our last battle, so I asked for a week's leave to visit the hospitals in Williamsburg and Yorktown. In Williamsburg, I attended meetings in the evening held by a minister from the Christian Commission for the Benefit of Wounded Soldiers. In several powerful sermons, the minister described the tender mercies of the Father and the love of the Son, Jesus. He preached Christ with such simplicity that many were moved to tears.

From Yorktown, I went down to White House Landing, a quiet little country village. After spending a day there, I was tired of idleness and ready to return to Fair Oaks. I boarded a train and whom should I see but the old peddler who spied on General McClellan for the Confederacy. At the station, I surprised him as he hobbled down the steps to the train platform. With the help of a nearby Federal soldier, we grabbed him and marched him to the Federal Provost Marshal. I quickly told him everything I knew about this Rebel spy. The Provost Marshal arrested him on the spot. The peddler glared at me as they hauled him away in chains.

No sooner did I return than there was another battle—this time at Gaines Mill. The surgeons and nurses could not keep up with all the wounded. Thank goodness men from the Christian Commission are here. They worked hour after hour alongside the surgeons. They dressed wounds, carried water to the thirsty, and spoke words of comfort to the dying. If a man was dying, they made sure he knew of the free gift of salvation given through Jesus Christ.

Your tired friend,

Emma

Richmond, Virginia

JULY 2, 1862

Dear Emma,

Wagon upon wagon brings more wounded and dead to the city. Charlie brings the papers over each day so Sissy can confirm that Lem is not listed as a casualty. She is desperate for word from him. Momma and I have been giving as much time as we can to nurse the wounded. There's no room left in the hospitals, so stores and homes are makeshift hospitals. Sissy and our boarders care for two soldiers in our home, while Momma and I work at Robertson Hospital.

Hundreds and hundreds of Yankee prisoners march to the prisons. I scan each of their faces to make sure yours is not among them.

I've had no messages lately, which is just as good. Mr. Simpson's store is filled with wounded Confederates. Not a good time to take a message to him to pass on to the Federals.

Are you wounded, Emma? Please send word as soon as possible.

Your worried friend,

Mollie Turner

Camp near Harrison's Landing

JULY 3, 1862

Dear Mollie,

I received my orders to ride to several hospitals to tell the surgeons, nurses, and those wounded who are able to walk to leave as quickly as possible. Ambulances couldn't reach them in time. The Union Army was retreating toward the James River, and soon their hospitals would fall into the hands of the Confederates.

I rode back as fast as possible through the hail of minnie balls falling around me. I kept glancing back over my shoulder and urging my horse to gallop faster. Suddenly, I saw a large group of Federal soldiers. I urged my horse on faster and raced towards them. When I came within a hundred yards of them, a soldier waved his hand to direct me another way. They were Federal soldiers all right, but they were guarded by a band of Rebels.

I pulled my horse up sharply and turned back just as another volley of minnie balls showered down in my path. I had no choice but to ride as hard and as fast as I could even though it was through a blaze of musketry and artillery. I have no idea how I made it. When I was past the range of the muskets, I pulled up on my horse. We were both slathered in sweat.

Nothing, *absolutely* nothing, but the power of the Almighty could have shielded me from such a storm of shot and shell and brought me through unscathed. It was for me as much of a miracle as that of Shadrach, Meshach, and Abednego coming forth from the fiery furnace without even the smell of fire upon them.

Your friend,

Emma

Richmond, Virginia

July 12, 1862

Dear Emma,

Another book and another message. This time when I unscrambled the message, it read, *basket of eggs.*

We have no chickens. Eggs have been scarce for months. The only place I've seen a basket of eggs was at Miss Van Lew's home. Surely she didn't mean for me to come to her house. She is Crazy Bet now, wandering around the prisons filled with Federal soldiers, singing her little ditties to herself, and scooping up lots of information while hospital and prison wardens laugh at her. Harmless old Bet. Crazy old Bet. Crazy like a fox, I say!

It was a warm day, so I sat outside on the veranda. Charlie came by just to let me know Richmond is safe under his watchful eye. He put his rusty musket in the corner and spread the newspapers out on the table. Of course, the papers say the Confederacy is winning, but I imagine the Washington papers say the Union is winning.

While we were sitting outside, a man pulled up in his hack. "Whoa!" he said to the horses and then hopped out. "Good day, Miss Turner."

Having no idea who he was, I said, "Good day, sir."

Then I noticed his peach pit pin. Wanting to warn him, I said, "This is Charlie. He is protecting our home front, but he really wishes he could be fighting for the Confederacy."

"Why, hello, young Charlie. Mrs. Simpson felt so badly about that jar of pickled peaches she sold to you that turned out to be rotten. She would like you to accept this basket of fresh eggs with her apologies."

I tried to sound natural while my heart was racing. "Thank you, and please thank Mrs. Simpson for me."

I took the basket inside, and told Charlie I'd be back in a moment with a cool drink for him. Once inside, I began to lift the eggs out of the basket and found one was as light as a feather. It

must be hollow. I held it up to the light and saw a message inside. I took it to my room and then returned to the veranda with a glass filled with Confederate lemonade for Charlie. Oh, for another lemon like Lem brought to us last month from the cavalry raid!

As soon as Charlie left, I broke open the egg. How clever of Miss Van Lew! Two small pieces of paper rolled up tight had been inserted through a narrow hole in the top of the empty egg shell. One was the coded message. I spread the other paper out next to my cipher and unscrambled the message. *Bandages. Store.*

I immediately knew what to do. I ripped part of the sheet from my bed and began to tear the cloth into strips. I rolled each one up into a bandage, but there was one that was tighter than the others to make sure the message inside did not show or slip out. I marked that bandage with a peach pit from the pickled peaches tied around it. I knew Mrs. Simpson would understand.

I walked down to the store with my basket of bandages. Mrs. Simpson moved around tending to the wounded with such gentleness, I realized that although her loyalties are with the North, her mother's heart is with these boys. I admired her for a few moments before I got her attention. "More bandages, Ma'am. Made them special for you." She nodded knowingly and took the basket full of bandages to the back of the store. I was sure she would find the single most important bandage in the basket.

A boy lifted his head and whispered, "Water." I found a ladle, scooped up some water from the bucket, and poured in gently into his mouth. His eyes signaled his appreciation as he slipped back into unconsciousness. Oh, Emma, when will this cruel war be over?

I simply must hear that you are safe. All this fighting around Richmond has kept even the private couriers from getting our letters to each other. I hope you have heard from me, and I hope I will hear from you soon.

Your friend,

Mollie

Richmond, Virginia

AUGUST 3, 1862

Dear Emma,

Sissy has decided to go to Baltimore and run the blockade, and I'm going with her. Sissy has it fixed in her head that she must make Lem a new uniform of Confederate gray wool with shining gold buttons. Lem has been promoted again, and Sissy insists he must have a uniform befitting his position. We all thought she was teasing at first, but the more Sissy turned the idea over in her head, the more determined she became. Thread, needles, Confederate gray wool, buttons, gold lace. All these are contraband articles, and the only way to get them is to make our way across Federal lines, purchase the goods in Baltimore, then run the blockade, and smuggle them back into Richmond.

At first, Momma objected, but then she has objected to every one of Sissy's adventures to see Lem. Once it was clear Sissy was going to run the blockade, Momma encouraged me to go with her because she thinks I can keep Sissy from being arrested, and she's worried about Great Auntie. We haven't heard from her in so long.

Momma has Confederate scrip for us to use until we get to the Federal line and gold to use once we're inside Federal territory. Momma sewed some false pockets inside our petticoats for hiding the gold. It will weigh us down, but it's the only medium of exchange for purchasing contraband goods. I think Momma would like us to get a few items for her too. She hasn't said anything yet, but I see the gleam in her eye when she hears Sissy talk about new needles and thread.

I sent a coded message to Miss Van Lew to let her know my plans and that I won't be available to pass on messages for a while. I took the message to Mrs. Simpson, and she agreed to pass it on.

I desperately want to be with Great Auntie. I've missed her so much. That alone is worth the risk.

Your adventurous friend,

Mollie

Richmond, Virginia

AUGUST 15, 1862

Dear Emma,

We leave tomorrow. Early this morning, I received a visit from
Mr. Simpson. He brought a jar of pickled peaches for Momma and a
book for me. I took the book to my room and found another coded
message in the spine. But there was no message inside in our special
code. I looked all over the book but could find no other hidden
message. I flipped through the pages but they were unmarked. Then
I saw the title of the book: *The History of Baltimore*. Is this message
supposed to go to Baltimore? Who gets it? Where do I take it?

We had much to do, but I slipped away and walked to Mr. and
Mrs. Simpson's store. Mrs. Simpson greeted me and guided me to
the back storeroom. Her peach pit pin indicated it was safe to speak
to her. She spoke in hushed tones. "Mollie, Betty needs your help. She
has information she must get to a certain general. She tried to start it
out on the relay stations, but she is being carefully watched right now.

"She went out early last evening to bring the message to our
store, and a man passed by her and said, 'Going North tonight?' She
thought that was odd, so she started muttering to herself in her best
Crazy Bet manner. The man passed by her again and said, 'Going
North tonight?' but again Betty just walked on. It's a good thing she
did too. It turns out this was a Confederate officer in civilian clothes
trying to trap her. She must be extremely careful now. She has vital
information that must get to the right person across the lines, but
she fears her normal relay stations are being watched too."

"I have the message, but I don't know who is to get it," I
explained. "Miss Van Lew didn't say anything to me about who's
supposed to get the message or how I will get it to him."

"She'll let you know somehow. Now leave quickly before any of
the customers become suspicious. Godspeed."

When I left the store, guess who I saw walking around in

circles, singing little songs? That's right—Crazy Bet. She walked by me and bumped into me. Hard. It knocked off her hat, and as I stooped to pick it up, she grabbed it and muttered, "Get away from me, girl." I stood staring at her as she continued down the street singing to herself. She said nothing about the book, a message, or who was to get it. A bystander clucked his disapproval. I kept looking back at her and was anxious for some sign or clue. After all, we're leaving for Baltimore in the morning. I puzzled about it all the way home until I put my hand in my pocket and found a small note, folded. I opened it and saw a message in our familiar code. I took out my cipher and solved the code: *Bakery. Charles St. Monday. Wednesday. Noon.*

Your faithful friend,

Mollie

Somewhere in Virginia

AUGUST 17, 1862

Dear Emma,

I'll have to bundle these letters together for a while until I'm in Federal land. Once inside the line, I will post them to you directly with United States stamps. Momma helped me make a false bottom to our trunk. I'm sure even the most diligent search won't reveal it. I'll keep these letters in there until it's safe to address them to you and mail them. Thank goodness for our invisible ink!

We took the train from Richmond and arrived at Culpeper yesterday. We stayed at a boarding house and shared a room with two other ladies. They also planned to run the blockade in Baltimore and had hired a wagon and driver. They had room for two more passengers and a couple of trunks. Sissy wanted to think about it, but I knew a good deal when I saw it.

Sissy was not at all assured when we saw our transportation. The wagon turned out to be an old cart with wide planks spread side by side across the axles with two chairs perched precariously in a large quantity of straw on the makeshift floor. When the two other ladies saw this royal carriage, they decided we were welcome to it and would wait until something suitable was available. Sissy and I both agreed that from what we could see, that could be a very long wait. Anything suitable had been confiscated for use by the army long ago.

We pushed our two small trunks up into the cart and then climbed up and tried to steady ourselves on the chairs. Giving up, we settled down in the straw. Our rugged driver snapped the reins and we were off. We stopped tonight at a ramshackle farmhouse. The farmer's wife was kind enough to us, though, and we slept on straw mattresses on the floor.

My body aches from the swaying of the wagon over the ruts in the road. I'm dreaming of Great Auntie's feather bed.

Your bone-weary friend,

Mollie

Top of the Blue Ridge Mountains

AUGUST 19, 1862

Dear Emma,

After another long day of travel in our wagon, our driver stopped at a small cottage and asked about lodging for the night. Sissy and I, weary from our travels, were more than ready to fall asleep, but the mountain woman gave us such a delightful supper of fresh eggs, milk, bread, and apple butter that we found ourselves renewed. We stayed up and talked with the dear woman for many hours. She was hungry for news of the war.

Before we left this morning, we walked to the top of the path on the hill. The early morning sun broke through a beautiful mist rising on the mountains. We could see miles and miles of breathtaking country — our Virginia — unstained by human blood, untouched by weapons of war. We were silent for quite some time, but I know both Sissy and I were thinking of happier times.

It was difficult to leave such a beautiful place. We insisted on paying for our lodging even when the woman protested. After all, we told our hostess, a good night's sleep after days of riding in that wagon was priceless!

Sissy gave me a look as she stepped up again into our special carriage. I think even she was beginning to wonder if a new uniform was worth all this agony. After another day in the wagon, we reached Berryville and yet another boarding house. Tomorrow will find us inside Federal lines. Sissy and I quietly rehearsed our story.

If anyone asks, we are worried sick about our great auntie in Baltimore who means so much to us. If asked our purpose for traveling without a pass from the War Department, we'll explain that our great uncle would have gotten us a pass, but as a surgeon for the wounded Union troops, he couldn't be located. If they check on us, they would surely verify that he was a Federal officer, just like them.

Tomorrow we cross the line.

Your daring friend,

Mollie

Berlin, Maryland

AUGUST 20, 1862

Dear Emma,

We crossed the Potomac River and our driver told us we were on our own. A boat crowded with Federal soldiers hugged the shore of Virginia. It was easy enough to secure passage on the boat, but whether we would be prisoners once on the Maryland shore was yet unknown. Sissy shook with fear, and I squeezed her hand. That kept one hand busy, but the other one twisted her curls over and over. If Sissy were a spy, she would never be able to keep secret messages hidden in her hair, for they would surely fall out with all her twisting.

I thought about my secret message and the letters to you. Last night, after Sissy fell asleep, I removed them from the false bottom in the trunk and sewed them up in my petticoat. Even though everyone, including girls, might be searched, I thought them safer there than in the trunk, which we knew for certain would be searched.

When we got to the Maryland shore, a Federal captain told us to wait. Sissy continued to shake, and I felt my mouth go dry. This had looked like a grand adventure on the other side of the river; now I'm not so sure. My heart pounded as I noticed that the Federals detained several others from the boat as well. A girl, about nine years old, clung to her mother. An older man, with a long beard, buried himself in his newspaper. A young man tapped his foot as his eyes darted back and forth. He seemed to me to have the most to lose in these interviews. Why would a man who could be fighting for either side stand there in civilian clothes wanting to cross without a pass? Could he be a spy too? Do I look as nervous and frightened as he does?

The captain asked each of us to declare who we were and what our purpose was in Federal lands. I tried to quiet my racing heart as I watched what was happening. The mother and child passed with flying colors. It seemed that the captain knew the woman's

husband, a Federal soldier. The woman and her daughter had
been caught behind Rebel lines visiting family as the battle lines
shifted. They were not searched, although their trunk was. Then
the captain interviewed the old man. He lived in Maryland, but had
taken his sick wife back to her family in Virginia before the war
started. There she had died, and he now needed to come back home.
He had papers showing he owned a home in Maryland. He too
quickly passed through without even having his trunk searched.

The captain spent twice as much time interviewing the nervous
young man. He said he was studying medicine in Baltimore. He
was returning to continue his studies after seeing his sister back
home to Virginia. I could tell the captain did not believe him. Both
his person and his trunk were searched, and he was detained for a
further interview with the marshal.

Now it was our turn. Sissy took a deep breath. She sat on her
hands to keep from twisting her hair. I drew in a sharp breath as
the captain asked me, "Young lady, where do you live?"

"Richmond ... with our momma."

His eyes narrowed, "And your father?"

"He died two years ago, and now it is just Momma, Sissy, and me."

"No brothers?"

I could tell he wanted to know where our fighting sympathies
fell so I said, "It is just us girls helping Momma with her boarders."

He turned to Sissy and asked, "Where are you traveling, and
what is your purpose in going there?"

"Dear captain, dear captain, you must help us!" Sissy exclaimed.
"We are desperately worried about Great Auntie. She lives in
Baltimore, and we have had no word from her in months. Momma
is beside herself and sent us to face whatever danger we must to find
out whether great auntie is well. She and Great Uncle Chester are all
we have left of Daddy. We must make sure she is safe." Tears poured
down Sissy's face, and I dabbed at her eyes with my handkerchief.

"Sir," I continued anticipating his next question, "our great uncle
is a Union officer. He was a doctor in Washington before the war and

offered his services to the Union as a surgeon at the beginning of the war. With so many battles and so many wounded, we have no idea where he is now. But you can check. In fact, you might be able to put us in touch with him. That would be very much appreciated. We want to see him too, but it is Great Auntie Belle we are most concerned about. She's alone in Baltimore. Great Uncle Chester moved her there months ago when Washington became an army camp."

I was shaking so hard, Sissy put out a hand to steady me. I was furious with myself. I'd poured out that explanation too quickly. I just knew he was on to me. Some spy I make. I can't even tell the truth about Great Auntie without looking guilty.

He made a few notes, and turned away. Sissy let out a big sigh, and I put my arm around her and squeezed her shoulder. I lowered my voice and whispered, "You were marvelous!" Sissy sat up a bit straighter, quite proud of her performance. I tried to look confident for Sissy's sake, but something just didn't feel right.

The captain returned with word that the marshal would check out our story, but it would take time. We would not be able to leave until tomorrow morning at the earliest. What did that mean? Was there something we said that didn't ring true? Sissy seemed relieved, but I thought there was something more. The captain directed us to a boarding house where we could spend the night. Why this boarding house? Why now? Was this a boarding house for those suspected of crossing the line?

The family seemed nice enough—at first. At dinner, they talked about how many Southerners try to cross the line here at this part of the river. They told us most folks were turned back, especially if they are found with contraband. Sissy and I looked at each other, and I saw the fear in her eyes. We carried only gold for this part of the journey; but I could tell she was thinking about our return trip. She knows nothing about my letters to you or my secret message.

"Yep," the man said, "nothing like a good capture around here to liven things up. It's always fun to see the looks on the faces of Rebel folk who thought they could outsmart us—once they are locked up in jail." His two sons hooted in laughter and slapped their knees. The father jeered at us. I picked at my food, which suddenly tasted like straw.

The wife was none the better. When a man delivered our two small trunks to us, she smiled slyly and said, "I wonder what secrets you gals are a-carrying in there. Maybe you've got something in there you'd like to share with us? Rebel gold, perhaps?"

Sissy and I hauled the trunks to our room. We weren't about to leave them in the hallway. We heard this family's cackles, knee slaps, and sinister whispers as we closed the door to our room. *Morning will not come soon enough, if you ask me*, I thought. Once behind closed doors, we placed the trunks against the door so no one could come in and examine them. Our clothes were in disarray, but it was clear they had not discovered the false bottom in my trunk. Momma should be proud — she is as good a spy as you and me!

I don't think our sleep will be sweet tonight, but we have made it this far and, for that, we are thankful. Good night, dear Federal friend. I sleep in your territory tonight as you have slept in mine near Richmond.

Your friend,

Mollie

On the train to Baltimore

AUGUST 21, 1862

Dear Emma,

We awoke to strong rapping on the door this morning. Having slept in our clothes, we were downstairs in a flash. The captain told us the marshal granted us permission to go.

We were relieved as the train rolled out of the station until we realized that the marshal's deputy was sitting a few seats away. Was he following us? Sissy read a Federal newspaper, and I read the *History of Baltimore*. Both of us looked over our paper or book to see him looking over his newspaper watching us. Didn't they believe our story back at Berlin?

Although we were anxious, the train chugged along, and we hoped we'd get to Baltimore without any more trouble. Our hopes were dashed when a man got on at one of the stops, conferred with the deputy, and then glanced our way. We continued to act as if we were unconcerned, but Sissy grabbed my hand and my heart started pounding. The hair stood up on the back of my neck. A quick glance revealed the deputy was staring at us. I squeezed Sissy's hand tighter.

The marshal's deputy and the other man jumped out of their seats as we pulled into the next stop. They showed us their badges and asked us to leave the train. My heart sunk. We've been found out. They had us identify our trunks, then removed them from the train. We stood on the platform watching our train to Baltimore chug out of the station. Sissy and I looked at each other and didn't say a word. We each knew what the other was thinking. Had we come this close only to be sent back home or worse—imprisoned? My mind raced and my face flushed hotly. *What did they suspect? What could I say to convince them there was nothing wrong? What if Sissy panicked and told them everything?*

The men escorted us to a small office in the train station. There we watched in silence as they searched our trunks again. Sissy

squeezed my hand so tightly, I thought I would cry out in pain. Only the pell mell thoughts of my frightened mind kept me focused on staying quiet. They patted the sides and tried to lift the bottom of Sissy's trunk. I held my breath as they searched my trunk and when they patted the bottom I was glad my letters were safely sewn into the lining of my petticoat. They found nothing.

Before I could relax, in walked a woman deputy to search our persons. She patted down Sissy's clothes and found our gold. Sissy said, "Momma gave it to us because Confederate notes certainly would not buy us train tickets to Baltimore." The deputy pocketed the small sack of gold and finished her search. As she walked off to the Provost office in the station, Sissy turned to me and said, "All is lost." She began to cry and I whispered sharply, "Stop it." Sissy was so surprised, she was quiet. Just in time too. The woman deputy returned empty-handed. It seemed we had lost our gold. Now what else was she looking for? Would we lose our freedom too?

I held my breath. She patted down my skirts but somehow missed the letters. But then she saw my book that I held in my arms the entire time. I took in a quick breath. This could be the end. Last night, concerned about the coded message, I had returned it to its original hiding place in the spine of the book. Even though it was a message for the Federals, I couldn't prove it because it was in code. If discovered, they might think I was spying for the Confederacy. I wouldn't want to have Miss Van Lew vouch for me and compromise her network of secret spies. I prayed that what had worked time and time again to get messages in and out of Libby Prison would work once more.

I began to prattle on about the book and how I was learning so much about Baltimore and its history and that my great auntie would be so proud and that she always wanted me to know more about Northern things. The searcher flipped through the book, turned it upside down, and shook it. Satisfied, she returned it to me, and I clutched it all the tighter.

Once again we had to tell our story, and once again Sissy performed remarkably well. You would have thought Great

Auntie Belle was on her deathbed, and we were the only ones in the universe who could save her. Finally, the deputy and the new marshal gave us back our gold and waved us on.

We waited four hours on the train platform for the next train to Baltimore. It was only when we boarded the train that we both broke down. Both of us shook so hard we thought we might throw the train off its tracks. All the way to Baltimore, Sissy twisted her hair, but I said not one word. I could certainly forgive her nervous habit this time!

Your exhausted friend,

Mollie

Baltimore, Maryland

AUGUST 22, 1862

Dear Emma,

Oh the joy we felt when we hugged Great Auntie. We couldn't wait to get to her home. We stayed up until three o'clock in the morning talking and laughing. Great Auntie exclaimed over and over, "My adventurous girls!" She didn't even seem to mind that Sissy's purpose in running the blockade was to secure cloth, thread, and buttons for a Confederate uniform. Great Auntie is so pleased with Sissy's courage that she said she'll do everything she can to help her get those contraband goods.

I went to sleep happy and tired, but with other things on my mind as well. Now that we were safe in Baltimore, I had to deliver the message to Miss Van Lew's contact at a bakery on Charles Street. Another day passed while the message stayed in the spine of my book. I worried I was too late. I wish I knew what this message said. Or who I was supposed to give it to. How would I get to the bakery without arousing suspicion with Great Auntie or Sissy? I fretted over this for a good long time before I could get to sleep.

Today, however, I knew I was not to make it to the bakery. Great Auntie had planned out our entire day and to suggest anything different would have made her wonder what I was up to. So today, I didn't think about messages, secret codes, or the war. Today I shopped!

Do you know how long it has been since I've been in a store with hats and clothes and ribbons and lace? Great Auntie took Sissy and me to the shops on Charles Street. I spotted the bakery and made a mental note of it, but since it isn't Monday or Wednesday, I decided to put spying out of my mind for the day. We were like two kids in a candy store. We touched the beautiful silk dresses. We tried on hat after hat. I purchased one for myself even though Sissy told me I would never be able to smuggle such a large item back through

enemy lines. The shopkeeper said these hats are all the rage in Paris now.

I knew we girls would get good use out of this hat if I could just get it back to Richmond. Besides, it would fold, so perhaps smuggling it through was not out of the question. As Great Auntie said, what's the worst that could happen? It would be confiscated, and I'd lose the money I had spent on it. That was a small enough risk to me. I may have a good head on my shoulders, but sometimes this good head likes to look pretty!

Baltimore is not at all like Richmond. Shops here are for shopping, not makeshift hospitals. People greet each other with hellos and good-days and tips of their hats. It reminds us of Richmond before the war.

There are men in Federal uniforms everywhere. That doesn't bother me, as you know where my loyalties lie. Sissy, however, was skittish. The few times we bumped into a Federal soldier on the street, she was downright terrified.

At the end of the day, we stopped for a pastry and some tea at a hotel. Real tea. With sugar. I sipped my tea slowly to treasure the smooth taste for as long as I could. I must try to bring some tea back for Momma. It was a day for girlish fun in girlish ways and something we have missed for so long in this interminable war.

Your friend,

Mollie

Baltimore, Maryland

AUGUST 23, 1862

Dear Emma.

After our shopping, we came back to Great Auntie's home and laughed until we cried. Sissy and I both are worn out with the war and Great Auntie seemed to know that. She let us both pile into her feather bed with her that night and snuggle close. We slept like babies.

This morning, I asked Great Auntie if Sissy and I could go to the bakery on Charles Street that I spied yesterday during our shopping to purchase some sweet rolls for our breakfast. We jumped at the chance to get out again with such freedom. Sissy and I skipped along the streets and giggled like little girls.

When we got to the bakery, the baker asked us to wait a moment because he had to pull his pies out of the oven. Sissy and I wondered if we could spare some of our precious money to purchase a pie. Even Sissy's hoard of sugar has been gone for months now. We licked our lips thinking about the sweet juices of a berry pie.

"Sorry to keep you so long, ladies," the baker said, "but with the rations, I can only bake pies on Mondays, Tuesdays, and Wednesdays. What can I get for you?"

While Sissy conducted the business, I stared at the baker. He seemed kindly, like Mr. Simpson. I asked him, "Do you like pickled peaches?" He look surprised, and muttered, "Never had them," and returned to his baking. I puzzled about it all the way home. How in the world am I supposed to get this message to the right person? I have no plan and Miss Van Lew didn't give me any clues on what to do once I got here. I've got to deliver the message while I am here, but how? And to whom?

Great Auntie was thrilled with our pie and said we should slice it very thin so that it would last all week. After breakfast, she announced we were going to a special tailor's shop. She would

forget her Yankee sensibilities for the day to assist Sissy in her venture.

The tailor kept materials for Confederate uniforms hidden in his backroom. He whispered, "I have to be very careful. The Yankees watch me. Come with me. I have several pieces of excellent Confederate cloth. Who is this for?"

Sissy said, "Kind sir, my husband is a captain and has just been promoted again. He must look the part of such a grand officer."

The tailor said, "Indeed! How do you plan to carry this cloth back across the lines?"

Great Auntie answered that we were waiting to obtain a pass from the War Department and sail on the flag-of-truce boat to Richmond.

He replied, "Then why don't you wear that uniform cloth right in front of those Yankee patrols!" Seeing the surprise on our faces, he explained, "I'll cut the cloth into proper lengths for you to make the uniform. Then I'll stitch those panels for you and your sister to wear home under your birdcage skirts."

Sissy and I looked at each other and grinned. "Just like Hetty!"

He seemed so pleased with himself, but then his face darkened. "Oh dear," he mumbled. "These buttons are another matter. They clearly state they are Confederate army. "Hmmm …" he said, "I shall cover them with wadding and cloth for you to button the panels like petticoats to your skirts!"

Sissy asked for enough plaid flannel to make Lem a new shirt. "Hmmm," he said again. Our tailor tapped his temple as if he were willing an idea to jump out of his head. Then suddenly his face brightened. "Shawls! I will make two plaid shawls from enough material to cut into shirts when you return."

I asked, "Isn't it a bit warm for shawls?"

"Yes," he replied, "but along the water at night, it will be cool. You will have need of them."

Great Auntie chimed in, "I plan to accompany them by the flag-of-truce boat, so make a shawl for me as well." We all laughed and then shushed each other—three ladies and their tailor in a grand conspiracy.

"Now, needles and thread, and gold lace for the uniform," reminded Sissy. The tailor had ideas for that as well as he studied Great Auntie's rather large purse. He asked if she could leave it with him. When she picked it up, the bottom would have new lining with the lace and needles and thread all folded smooth and sewn up inside.

A marvelous day! You see, Emma, we too have a disguise! We're three ladies who will be wearing a Confederate uniform in front of everyone—but no one will know. Now if only I could have as much success with my message.

Your friend,

Mollie

Washington, D.C.

AUGUST 26, 1862

Dear Mollie,

Our men were discouraged to turn away from Richmond. We were so close. Our regiment marched to Newport News and then on to Aquia Creek. We weren't there long before we were off to support General Pope's army in the Shenandoah Valley. I wished I could've been with them, but I was needed for other secret missions. My job as Regimental Postmaster gives me much freedom and cover for these missions. Yet, as much as I enjoy these missions, I miss my unit, and my talks with James.

I've now had four assignments behind enemy lines, but this was my most memorable one. General Heintzelman wanted me to go behind enemy lines and get information about the enemy's troops. This time, I disguised myself as a female slave. I wore a straw hat that came down over my eyes and hid half my face. I wasn't going to make the same mistake as last time of someone looking at my face and thinking I wasn't a slave. Once I crossed the Rebel lines, I joined a group of nine slaves who serve the needs of the Rebel army. A Rebel officer ordered me to headquarters to prepare their meals.

The Rebels speak openly about their troops and their plans. The Federals keep maneuvers and locations of troops a secret from the soldiers. But here, all you have to do is be in the right place, listen, and remember what you hear.

It didn't take long for me to hear the officers discussing their plans for the next day. At first they spoke in low tones, but then they became excited and, forgetting us slaves, spoke freely. They even mentioned the number of reinforcements and when they would arrive.

The next morning, I cooked breakfast with the other slaves. As I moved a campstool that stood in my way, I saw some official-looking papers sticking out of the pockets of a Confederate coat laid over the stool. I quickly grabbed them and stuffed them into my

own pockets, hidden in the dress I wore. I left before anyone noticed the documents were missing. I hoped it was a map or a battle plan or something useful to our cause, but I couldn't risk looking at them until I got away.

I crept toward the picket line that was nearest to the Federals, made my way to an old house, and hid in the cellar. Within moments, the Federals and the Rebels began firing at each other. Cannon balls and minnie balls rained down. Suddenly, something struck the old house. Wood splintered and stone shattered. I screamed and covered my head with my arms. There was nothing I could do as the volleys came in waves. I had to wait until it was over. Suddenly, part of the floor above me fell into the cellar. I couldn't breathe for all of the dust and dirt that fell over me. I thought this was the end.

I closed my eyes and remembered good old Elijah who remained in the cave during the tempest, the earthquake, and the fire. Only when he'd heard the still small voice of the Lord, did he venture out. I waited and waited for the still small voice. I know that the Lord is my sure refuge and could protect me in this crumbling house in the midst of a battlefield as well as any parlor in a city. The small still voice of the Lord coincided with the stilling of the muskets and the quieting of the cannons. The Rebels fell back and took a new position. Assured this was the right time, I escaped quickly over into Federal lines.

I raced to headquarters and reported the facts I had overheard. I pulled out the documents and handed them to General Heintzelman. Imagine my surprise to learn these were orders for the Confederate commanders with instructions for how and when to move to capture Washington.

But they will not capture Washington now — will they!

Your determined Yankee friend
and soldier,

Emma

Baltimore, Maryland

AUGUST 27, 1862

Dear Emma,

Great Auntie gave us permission to go out again. Sissy wanted to find where Hetty Cary lived before she fled to Richmond, and I said I wanted to window shop. I knew I could slip away to the bakery for a midday treat without arousing any suspicion.

I arrived there at eleven o'clock. I took my time selecting a biscuit. I sat at a little table in the corner and slowly buttered my biscuit. That spot allowed me to be near the window and the entrance and directly under the clock.

The bakery filled with customers, some of whom seemed like regulars. The baker greeted many of them by name.

The clock chimed each quarter hour. I pretended to read my book — *The History of Baltimore*. At forty-five minutes after eleven, the clock chimed again and a Federal soldier, a captain, came in the store. He talked in low tones with the baker. Could he be the one? Yet, he left with his bread and hardly glanced in my direction.

I could hear the massive hands of the clock as they moved the space of each minute to noon. *Bong. Bong. Bong.* Yet no person — man or woman — appeared. *Bong. Bong. Bong.* Even the baker left the counter to tend his ovens. *Bong. Bong. Bong.* My book burned in my hands as I thought about the message inside it that I needed to get to the right person. *Bong. Bong. Bong.* Twelve strikes.

The door opened and a young man who looked about eighteen or nineteen years of age came into the store. He didn't even look my way. "Hmmm … hmmm. Smells awfully good in here!" he said to no one in particular.

He gazed into the cases, trying to make his selection. The baker asked, "Young Mr. Evers, what can I get you today?"

The young man smiled broadly and said, "Two cookies, sir." When he made his purchase, he walked over to my table, laid one of the cookies down on the table on a cloth napkin, and then, whistling to himself, he left the store.

I stared at the cookie. Was it a clue? Was there something written on the napkin? I turned the napkin over but found no writing in code or otherwise.

As I walked home, I replayed the scene over and over again in my mind. If it wasn't the baker or the soldier, could it be that young man, Mr. Evers? He seemed nice enough, but if he was the one, then why did he make contact with me and then leave the bakery? It made no sense. I walked home dejected. Wednesday noon had come and gone, and now there would be no chance to meet my contact again until next Monday. Emma, what if this message was urgent? What if Great Auntie gets us a flag-of-truce boat before next Monday?

Oh, Emma, this spy business is not so easy after all.

Your discouraged friend,

Mollie

Baltimore, Maryland

AUGUST 29, 1862

Dear Emma,

I simply had to put it out of my mind. It looks like Great Auntie's arrangements for us to travel by a flag-of-truce boat have hit some problems. Great Auntie was trying to get a particular boat where she knows the captain. She hoped that would help us smuggle our contraband through the blockade easier. She found out today that we won't be able to sail on that boat. She's been told the earliest we will leave is next Monday. She looks worried. I've been having so much fun here with Great Auntie and Sissy that I haven't given much thought to the last part of our journey—actually running the blockade with our smuggled contraband. Great Auntie shooed me out of the room and made light of the change. Yet, I see how she is fiddling with her apron. She's definitely worried.

I'd almost forgotten what fun was like. Today, Great Auntie, Sissy, and I went to the theater and a concert, and Great Auntie introduced us to her new friends. They were surprised when we told them what Richmond was like now.

The best time we had with Great Auntie was when we told her about Daddy's letters. I noticed Sissy did not share what was in hers, and I certainly did not share what was in mine. There would be time for that later, when I could tell Great Auntie the whole story and how Daddy's letter affected my decisions about certain things related to this great war.

Sissy and I have worked hard for so long—sewing uniforms, rolling bandages, nursing the wounded, and caring for boarders. We thoroughly enjoyed being taken care of by Great Auntie. I think she enjoyed it too, for she pampered us exquisitely. I wish Momma could've been here to enjoy a rest from her labors.

Tomorrow, Great Auntie is holding a reception in our honor. She has invited a number of young ladies and young men to make our

acquaintance. It's too late for Sissy, but Great Auntie still holds out hope that I'll marry a Northerner. She told me she's invited several young medical students from Johns Hopkins to attend.

"Younger versions of Great Uncle Chester?" I inquired sweetly.

"You could do worse," she responded.

Of course, that was all Sissy needed to inspire another shopping trip. She had carefully counted out the gold she had remaining after paying for Lem's uniform and shirts. With some additional funds provided by Great Auntie, we three were off again shopping for new dresses. I almost felt guilty, as I knew these funds could be spent on medicine and food, but Great Auntie insisted both of us have a new dress for the party. "Even if we can't smuggle them back," Great Auntie insisted, "I shall keep them here for you until the end of the war." It was frivolous, extravagant, and oh so appreciated!

Sissy and I had the time of our lives trying on the latest fashions. We finally made our selections, and Great Auntie paid to have them delivered to her home. We then went to tea at the hotel around the corner from the bakery.

The lobby was filled with Federal soldiers, many of whom were officers. Great Auntie conversed easily with the ones she knew. They asked about Great Uncle Chester, to which she always replied, "Mending you boys as fast as he can!" Sissy shifted in her seat. I know she felt she was disloyal to the Confederacy for sipping delicious tea—with sugar—in a hotel populated with Federal officers. I squeezed her hand under the table so that she would know I understood.

I'm the one who is disloyal to the Confederacy. I'm the one who takes the messages from one Federal agent to another. Yet, in my heart, I know it's the right thing to do. We must preserve the Union and that Union must be free of slavery.

I count the minutes until Monday at noon.

Your friend,

Mollie

Baltimore, Maryland

AUGUST 30, 1862

Dear Emma,

It's very late, but I must stay up to write you. Tonight, Great Auntie held the reception here at her home for Sissy and me. She introduced us to many wonderful young people. It took me back to a time several years ago when there was a similar reception for Sissy and me at our cousin's in Connecticut — a time when I met a young man named Franklin Thompson, a Bible salesman. Ah! But he was not what he seemed. He was a she. You trusted me with your secret then and now. I thank God for the friendship that developed between us.

It is very complicated, and I don't pretend to understand it all, but this one thing I know. Very committed, caring people on both sides of this war believe they are right and believe God will vindicate their position. But how can the South win if it stands for slavery? How much longer can God permit our country to enslave those he created, and call them *our property!* I do pray this war is over soon and that the entire country will agree on this question of slavery.

At the reception tonight, like so much in this war, music and dancing and laughter and fun were ours to enjoy until we heard the news. At the second battle of Manassas, the Federals were barely holding their lines just miles from Washington. Everyone fell silent at the party. Everyone knew that if Washington was captured, Baltimore was not far away. And, if Washington fell to the Confederates, then the great experiment of the United States was over.

Sissy should have been glad for the Confederate victory, but she whispered to me in a plaintive voice, "Lem ... I have to know if he's safe."

Great Auntie stopped the music and asked us to all join with her in a prayer for the men and boys in the field. I know she was thinking of her husband and whether he was on duty on the battlefield. Sissy was thinking of Lem and whether or not he was wounded, and I, of course, as always, silently but prayerfully thought about you, my dear disguised soldier in blue.

May God be with you, Emma.

Your friend,

Mollie

Baltimore, Maryland

SEPTEMBER 1, 1862

Dear Emma,

It's Monday. Today's the day. Noon at the bakery. I have Great
Auntie's permission to buy a pie, and I'm counting down the
minutes until time to leave.

✳ ✳

Emma, I wrote the lines above this morning, but I had no idea
I wouldn't be able to finish this letter until late at night. At eleven
o'clock today, as I prepared to leave for the bakery, a Federal officer
appeared at our doorstep. Great Auntie nearly fainted for she was
afraid it was bad news about Great Uncle Chester. The young officer
assured her he was there to provide details on the passage on the
flag-of-truce boat that was leaving first thing in the morning from
the harbor.

He told us what we would be permitted to bring and that our
persons and our belongings would be searched. He leveled his eyes
at Sissy and me and added, "Anyone found with contraband will be
summarily removed from the boat." Sissy held her breath and her
face was calm. Only the twisting of a strand of hair gave her away.
Yet, she quickly stopped the twisting and stood up straight. I could
see the fire in her eyes and the determination in her spirit. She
didn't come this far for Lem's uniform to leave without it!

Great Auntie said I had no time for the bakery, and that sweets
on a flag-of-truce boat would be confiscated anyway as contraband.
She then directed Sissy and me to tend to a long list of things
we had to do to be ready by seven tomorrow morning. My list
had nothing to do with going down to Charles Street, and it was
already eleven forty-five. I would return to Richmond with my
message as surely as I had left with it.

Suddenly, Sissy said, "Great Auntie! We have to pick up your
purse, the one with the needles and threads and gold lace for Lem's

uniform. The tailor delivered the shawls and our gray petticoats, but he forgot to send the purse."

I jumped at the opportunity. "I'll go—quick as lightning. Why, I'll be back before the clock strikes one." Great Auntie agreed, and I rushed to Charles Street. I carried my book under my arm, which thankfully, Great Auntie and Sissy were too distracted to notice.

I nearly ran the entire way and arrived at the store just as the clock began to strike noon. My eyes darted to each customer. No one even glanced in my direction. If it were Mr. Evers, he was not there yet. Twelve bongs sounded and no Mr. Evers. I shifted my weight from one foot to the other. Fifteen more minutes passed with no sign of Mr. Evers. Customers continued to come in, make their purchases, and leave. My heart raced as I sat and watched the clock tick by fifteen more minutes. As the clock struck the half hour, I could not wait any longer. I stood to leave just as Mr. Evers jauntily strode into the store. He tipped his hat to me, and said, "No cookie today?"

I had to find out if he was the one. "I much prefer pickled peaches," I replied.

He laughed. "To cookies? During the war, when sweets are a treat? I would think a young Southern girl like you would want a cookie a day!"

How did he know I was Southern? I suppose it could have been my Virginia accent. Or perhaps he had some information from Miss Van Lew about me? He purchased two cookies and said, "Would you care to share one with me?"

I didn't have much time. I had to get to the tailor's shop and home before one o'clock. I impatiently nibbled at my cookie, wanting desperately for him to reveal himself to me. "I do not even know your proper name—to thank you—for the cookie, of course."

"Mr. Evers. Adam Evers. Formerly of Richmond. Now studying medicine in Baltimore. At your service, Miss ..."

"Miss Turner. Mollie Turner. Still of Richmond. Visiting Baltimore."

"Ah, I see you have a book about Baltimore. Could I see it?"

I clutched the book tightly. He could be the one, but I had to know for sure. I handed him the book and watched him steadily.

"Hmm … *The History of Baltimore.*" He looked inside and read a few sentences. Then he turned the book and stared at the spine. He turned the book to me with the spine facing me, tapped the spine, and said, "I imagine that this book is filled with secrets about this old city."

Was he trying to tell me something?

"Secrets that would take quite a historian to decipher," he continued.

Decipher! He must be the one, I thought.

"I fancy myself a historian. I would love to read this book. Might I borrow it?"

I stared steadily at him. He seemed to know there might be a secret message in the spine of the book, but how could I be sure he was the one?

"And how, pray tell, would you return it to me? There's been no mail between the North and South for more than a year."

"Why, Miss Mollie, I would commandeer the flag-of-truce boat and take it to you myself!"

We both laughed at such an idea.

"Then," I asked, "how would you find me when you got to Richmond?"

"Well, first I would stop by Jeff Davis' home and inquire where the most beautiful girl in Richmond lived. But if he couldn't tell me, I would go to a delightful shop on Main Street and inquire about the young lady who always purchases pickled peaches and returns only the pits."

He knew about Mr. and Mrs. Simpson and their shop on Main Street. He knew about the peach pit sign, though he did not wear one now.

"Then you must read this book," I said. "By all means, read it cover to cover. Let nothing escape your attention. Then and only then will you know what I know." Assured that my mission was successful, I rose from the table. Adam Evers opened the door for me. I turned to wave good-bye, but he had already slipped out the door. The handsome and mysterious young Mr. Evers was gone from my life.

I hurried to the tailor's shop and picked up the purse. First, the tailor showed me the very fine work he had done in the lining. I felt all around the bottom, but could find no evidence of the needle or thread or gold lace. I thanked him and hurried home with both missions accomplished.

The rest of the day, Great Auntie barked orders at Sissy and me. I don't think you or Lem have a tougher drill sergeant than the one we had today. She made sure we had our outfits, our trunks, and our stories all shipshape before bed.

Great Auntie is firmly in charge of our venture home, and told us to follow her lead tomorrow. Frankly, with all that Sissy and I have been through the last few weeks, we were happy to follow whatever orders she gave. We packed our trunks carefully. It would not do for Great Auntie to be accused of assisting Confederate girls to smuggle contraband goods through the lines, especially when she had used Great Uncle Chester's rank and reputation to secure the passes for us from the War Department.

Sissy looked at her new dress longingly and then packed it away in a drawer at Great Auntie's home. I stared at my hat a very long time. I thought and thought and thought about how to get it back with me. We were already heavy laden with our petticoats that concealed the Confederate gray cloth and buttons for Lem's uniform, and our new shawls made out of flannel for Lem's shirts. Great Auntie insisted that I leave it, and with great sadness I bid the lovely hat adieu.

I hadn't told Great Auntie, but I had added some tea and coffee in the false bottom of my trunk. I wanted something for Momma, and she does so love her coffee. If only I could have hidden some sugar to go with it. I checked again to make sure that the false bottom was secure so that Momma could have a reward for her troubles. I included extra needles, pins, buttons, and threads for

Momma. I must get these things through for her. They all fit nicely under the false bottom of the trunk.

Sissy fell asleep early. I settled in next to Great Auntie on the sofa. Great Auntie, all tuckered out from her day of bellowing orders, slowly sipped her cup of tea with sugar, a Federal luxury she would soon be without. "Child, if only Chester could see you now. Soon the boys will come courting. That is, of course, once they come home from the war. I wonder whom you will marry, dear. It will have to be someone full of adventure—someone with integrity and spirit. Someone like your great uncle, I do imagine."

"I miss him so much, Great Auntie. When will we be able to see him again?"

She sighed. "I think that is the question of the long war. When, oh when, will it be over?"

Your friend,

Mollie

Manassas, Virginia

September 3, 1862

Dear Mollie,

We met the enemy again at Bull Run. This time we were stronger and more experienced, and we were ready. But, Mollie, we were soundly trounced.

During the fighting, the commanding generals ordered me behind Rebel lines four times over a ten-day span. I moved back and forth along the lines observing the troops and their artillery and then reporting to headquarters. The last, during the Battle of Chantilly, was the worst.

The night of the battle, as I edged my way back to the Federal lines, a soldier rode up to the picket line. I thought he was a Rebel officer until the Rebel pickets fired at him. The soldier fell from his horse. When the Rebel pickets realized they had killed a Federal general, they shouted for joy. But when I heard it was General Kearney, I fell to my knees.

While the attention of the pickets was drawn in another direction, I lost no time in my escape. I reported to headquarters, where Colonel Poe ordered me to take certain dispatches and documents to General McClellan. I rode as fast as I could to Washington. General Lee comes closer to Washington. I have even heard there is a warship anchored in the Potomac to take away President Lincoln and his cabinet members if the capital should fall to General Lee.

When I returned, I hurried to find James. He knew of the death of General Kearney. I fought back tears as I told James I would have willingly died in General Kerney's place to save such a great general in the Union Army. "A noble thought, Frank," James said, "but the Union Army needs you too."

"It's not noble, James. I may have the same devotion to the Union as the general, but I certainly lack the skill to accomplish

what he did. If I were to fall, another nurse would be appointed in my place, but General Kearney ... who can replace him?"

James replied, "Frank, this war will be won by the sacrifice of many little-known Union soldiers. I understand your desire to have offered your life to save the great general, but it is the far greater sacrifice to offer your life now for those who have no voice and who seem to others nothing more than worthless property. The little-known Union soldier does that every day in this war, Frank."

I suppose he's right, but even the little-known Union soldier likes to have a hero to lead him into the battle. I will miss General Kearney terribly.

Your friend,

Emma

Fort McHenry, Baltimore

Dear Emma,

When we arrived to board the flag-of-truce boat, the Federal officers locked us in together to wait while they searched the baggage. Mothers who risked everything and spent their last dollar on shoes for their children wailed as soldiers confiscated the shoes. Soldiers stripped necessities for life from women who were just trying to help their families survive. Needles, pins, thread, cloth, sugar, coffee, tea, lemons, and limes were all taken. Sissy looked at me. I knew she was thinking of the confederate cloth hidden in our clothes.

Then it was our turn to be searched. The woman who conducted our search seemed bored with the task and barely bothered searching Great Auntie's and Sissy's clothes. I prayed silently that the inspector would be just as disinterested when searching mine. The woman made Sissy undo her hair to see if she had any contraband left there. As Sissy turned to undo her hair, she looked at me with fear in her eyes. In an instant, I realized what Sissy was thinking. The message in my hair!

This morning I showed Sissy what to expect from the search. I was so happy about the success of my mission that I got careless. I grabbed Miss Van Lew's coded message to me and said to Sissy, "Pretend I'm a spy and I have a secret message. This is how those female spies got messages to our Confederate generals." I rolled the coded message up in my hair and fastened it with hair pins on the top of my head. Sissy laughed and said I looked every bit as innocent and beautiful as the spy who carried the message from Rose Greenhow's Washington prison to Manassas last year. No one suspected the girl at all and she dismounted from her horse, unrolled her hair, and a message that turned the battle tumbled out.

It was silly fun, but now we both realized that in the hurrying

around this morning to get to the boat on time, I had not undone my hair. The coded message was still hidden there.

After the woman finished searching Sissy and Great Auntie, she patted down my clothes and found nothing. I breathed steadily trying to still the pounding in my heart. Sissy looked down at the floor. I think she was afraid the fear in her eyes would give me away. The inspector had me take off my shoes and shake them out. Satisfied, she stood back, and for a moment, I thought the search was over. Then she pointed to my hair neatly pinned up on my head, and said, "Unwind your hair." When I hesitated, her eyes narrowed and she came closer.

I met her eyes and did not flinch. "But madam, I worked so hard to fix my hair for my Momma in Richmond. I would so appreciate it if I might just leave my hair as it is."

"You'll have plenty of time on this trip to fix it again," she said as she reached for the hair pins. I pulled back. She ordered me to stand still. She pulled out the hair pins one by one until my hair—and its contents—fell down around my shoulders. "Guard," the woman shouted, "seize her!"

Sissy screamed, "No!"

The guard pushed me up to the deck. With a tight grip on my arm, he marched me off the ship directly to the Provost Marshal's office located at the harbor. The guard left me in a small locked room with a tiny window for several hours. I watched the flag-of-truce boat pull out of the harbor without me. At least Sissy and Great Auntie and our trunks would make it to Richmond.

When it was my turn to be interviewed by the Provost Marshal, I saw that he had the coded message in his hand. My mind raced as I tried to think what to say. "Young lady, what do you have to say for yourself?"

"It was just a game, sir. A silly game, and now it has landed me in terrible trouble, I realize that. Please let me explain. You see, my sister and I talked this morning about what the search would be like. We were pretending to be spies just like the ladies Mrs.

Greenhow used to get messages to the generals. I had this silly coded message—not meant for anyone else, sir—all tied up in my hair. In the excitement of getting ready for the boat, I forgot to get it out. My mistake, sir, but it's not a criminal mistake."

The Provost Marshal applauded. "Well done, Miss Turner. But it's not good enough for me. Perhaps an audience at Fort McHenry can appreciate your drama." He scribbled something on a piece of paper and gave it to the guard. An hour later when the guard turned me over to Fort McHenry, I saw the paper with my name, Mollie Turner, and two words handwritten by the Provost Marshal: *Rebel spy.*

I have been here six days now. Once inside the fort, I was thoroughly searched and the confederate gray cloth that made up my petticoat was discovered and confiscated. The guard who took me to my cell told me *blockade runner* is now added to my charges.

There are many Confederate soldiers imprisoned here, but a lot of other prisoners too who are imprisoned for charges that have nothing to do with fighting. There are legislators, doctors, chaplains, and newspaper editors. I have struck up a friendship with Mr. Stone, editor of the *The South*. His crime is none other than printing views favorable to the South. He gave me paper and ink. He told me he can't give me freedom of speech as that has all been taken away, but he can make it possible for me to be free to write. He slipped me a vial of special ink and told me to only record my secret thoughts with it. I know I can't get these letters to you right now—it's too dangerous. It is good to write to you though.

Six long days. The food isn't so bad. Twice a day we get bread, some gruel, and water. Now and then we get meat. The political prisoners (and now I am one!) seem to have more freedom than I would have expected. They can receive visitors (if only someone knew I was here!) and purchase supplies. There is a prisoner, a peddler of sorts, who is permitted to sell things to the political prisoners. Mr. Stone tells me this man used to go to Federal camps and sell newspapers, letter writing paper, ink, and food. What he

overheard he took to the Confederates and for that he was turned
in as a spy. Yet he has been here for a while now and caused no
trouble. The guards buy the supplies, which he then sells to the
political prisoners. The peddler gets his supplies for free and the
guards take the profit. It's a well-run business that meets the needs
of us all, I suppose.

I have no idea how long I will be here. Mr. Stone has been here
over a year with no trial, and he is not labeled a spy. What will they
do with me? If they think I'm a Rebel spy, I will be here forever! Or
worse! But I can't reveal Miss Van Lew as my source to convince
these people that I'm not a Rebel spy. It would risk her entire
network.

I miss Momma so much. I wish I hadn't been so stupid. Some
spy I make. Playing silly games and ending up in prison for the rest
of my life. This'll break Momma's heart. Sure I said I wanted to do
something important, something like you, but I was stupid, Emma.
Just plain stupid.

Mr. Stone tried to help me. He knows how discouraging it can
be to be locked up here. I think he's trying to help me keep my
mind off of things. He convinced the guard to let me attend French
lessons conducted by another political prisoner, a doctor. There are
several chaplains who conduct worship services and Mr. Stone told
me of a weekly debating club that he attends with several other
doctors and newspapermen.

I'm not the first female to be imprisoned here. Mr. Stone said
another lady was here for seven months charged with spying and
carrying Rebel mail. I asked him what happened to her after she
was here, but he didn't know. Some guards spit in my cell, which
scares me, but others are civil and well-behaved. Mr. Stone says I
remind him of his daughter and that he'll watch over me.

His daughter visits him twice a week. She brings him writing
paper and ink and secret ink powder hidden inside the lining of her
hat. Mr. Stone mixes the secret ink powder with his drinking water
to create an invisible ink. He has asked her for a double portion now

that I'm here, and she's agreed to try to smuggle it in. The guards monitor what writings he sends out with his daughter, but they are not aware that his rambling journal about prison life in Fort McHenry is a foil for the hidden invisible writings on the back side of the pages. His daughter helps him write articles for a Confederate paper this way. He said that maybe he can get a letter out to my family by way of his daughter. In the meantime, I'll keep writing you even though I have no idea if I will ever see you again or even be able to get these letters to you.

It is a strange thing to make new friends with prisoners in this fort. Not at all what I expected when this adventure with Sissy began. I was supposed to keep her out of jail. Now look at me.

Your captured friend,

Mollie

Fort McHenry, Baltimore

SEPTEMBER 10, 1862

Dear Emma,

The peddler came by my cell this morning. He makes my skin crawl, Emma. There is something about him. Call it intuition, but I'm going to be on guard around him. He asked me if I wanted to buy any of his wares. Of course, I have no money since the remaining gold sewn up in my skirts was taken as well. I politely told him no, thank you, but he lingered to talk.

"A Rebel spy, hmmm," he said. "I'm a Rebel spy too, you know. Who did you take your secrets to?" I stared at the floor. "What kind of secrets did you carry?" I still said nothing. "Certainly a young girl like you would have had help. Whose network did you belong to? I know most of them, you know."

I wanted him to go away, and being quiet wasn't doing the trick. "Well, sir, I was wondering. I heard you were a formidable spy with many missions before you were caught. What, pray tell, landed you in here?"

"A tattletale, that's what! A whimpering no-good slip of a soldier, just a boy, who said he had proof that I was not what I seemed. Why, I was the old peddler who brought him his writing paper and news many times in his camp. He knew that, but when I was on the train, he took advantage of old Jim and turned me in. You know what I think, young lady? I think he is the spy. Else, how would he know I was in the Federal camp and then in the Rebel camp telling secrets, hmmm? Yep, that's what I think. He's the real spy."

He muttered something about old Jim's revenge if he ever got out of there and stomped down the hall. Good riddance. He sends shivers down my spine. I'd much rather get my supplies through Mr. Stone's kindness than pay a cent to that man.

Your friend,

Mollie

Fort McHenry, Baltimore

September 12, 1862

Dear Emma,

Mark today down! A wondrous day! I have found a way to make myself useful, earn some money and good will, and get myself out of this dreary cell. I am nursing the patients in the hospital ward.

I told Mr. Stone about my days of nursing at Robertson Hospital. Captain Sally's fame goes far. Mr. Stone passed this information on to his doctor friends in the prison debating club. The doctors are impressed with Captain Sally and that I knew her. They asked lots of questions about my time at Robertson Hospital, which I eagerly answered. It's always fun to tell stories about Captain Sally. It reminded me of a time at another prison—Libby.

Today one of the doctors was pressed into service in the hospital ward, just as I was telling another story about Captain Sally. The doctor told the guard that he wished to have my services too. I pleaded with the guard to let me go with the doctor. I told him that if I did not prove myself useful within one hour, he could march me right back to my cell and take away my French club privileges. The guard smiled and said that wouldn't be necessary, but he would take me with him to see if Dr. Bruden, the doctor in charge of the prison hospital ward, had any use for me.

I knew exactly what to do. (Thank you, Captain Sally!) I quickly went about my duties, changing linens and bandages. Adopting Captain Sally's standards for cleanliness, I made sure the beds, the wounded prisoners, and the bandages were sparkling clean. I washed all the surgeon's tools and when I asked for soap to clean them, Dr. Bruden raised an eyebrow. "Captain Sally always washed up with soap and her charges hardly ever died. I think it is the secret to her success, and if you don't mind, I aim to be just as successful as she was."

Dr. Bruden found me particularly useful in cheering the

prisoners and efficient in my nursing duties. He has agreed that I can help out in the hospital ward every day, and even put in an order of soap with the Provost Marshal. I'm exhausted but happy. The days will pass more quickly now.

Your friend,

Mollie

Fort McHenry, Baltimore

SEPTEMBER 15, 1862

Dear Emma,

I missed my French lesson today, but was happy to be useful in the prison hospital. The men are in great need of nursing. Dr. Bruden let me read the Scriptures to a young solder as he was laboring for his last breaths. There was no time to get the chaplain. This young man's only charge was not being willing to take the oath of allegiance to the Federal government. Yet he has been here a year, unbending in his decision to stay loyal to the Confederacy. Strong opinions on both sides, Emma. Opinions worth fighting for, I suppose.

Emma, you have seen so much death up close. I have seen none—until today, that is. Captain Sally almost never lost a patient and certainly never one while I was there. As I read to him and watched him struggle for a breath, tears began to slip down my cheeks. I wiped them away and tried to focus my eyes. I certainly wanted to read the Scriptures for this young man. Dr. Bruden kept a watchful eye on me. I read a verse, then wiped away my tears, then read another verse. Finally, when the young man breathed his last, I fell over him and sobbed. I thought of his mother. Then of my own. I miss Momma so much.

A prison guard gently pried my hands from the Bible and led me back to my cell. I could not sleep at all. I am so lonely, and so sad.

Today, Dr. Bruden told me he was glad I was there to help that young man. I suggested to Dr. Bruden that he let me go bed to bed to read Scriptures and pray for the men. I told him it was a technique Captain Sally used that seemed to cheer the men, give them hope, and help them focus on being whole again. Dr. Bruden's eyebrow shot up again. He turned away, but I heard him tell the guard to let me keep the Bible.

After my duties, I took the Bible and sat by as many of the

wounded and sick in the ward of about thirty men as I could before the guard required me to return to my cell. Captain Sally was right. Reading the Bible to the men and praying with them is a good medicine—for the soul and for the body as well. The men in the ward seemed in much better spirits when I left them tonight. I said a prayer for Captain Sally tonight. I am glad she taught me well.

Your friend,

Mollie

Fort McHenry, Baltimore

September 18, 1862

Dear Emma,

The fort shook yesterday with the sounds of cannons in the distance that sounded like thunder. A stillness pervaded the prison. All strained to hear the sounds of battle. Later we got the news of a terrible battle near Sharpsburg, Maryland, just fifty miles from here. We still don't know who won. Casualties were high, Mr. Stone told me — on both sides. Were you fighting there? Oh, Emma, I do wish I could get your letters. One day you shall have mine. I'm saving them for you. It helps me just to write to you.

The guard told me that Fort McHenry will receive many of the wounded soldiers who will begin to arrive by ambulance train soon. He said I was needed in the hospital ward to prepare the surgeon's tools and ready the beds. Those prisoners who were well enough to be moved were helped to their cells. It was late tonight before I returned to my cell. Tomorrow, the wounded arrive. I pray I do not see your face.

Your friend,

Mollie

Baltimore, Maryland

SEPTEMBER 20, 1862

Dear Mollie,

The sound of the crack of muskets and the boom of cannons signaled that the fighting had begun. During this time, the doctors and nurses stood by. All we could do was wait for the first to fall and then rush to tend them. Mollie, waiting for the wounded to fall is the worst part of my duties.

Not even what I saw at Fair Oaks compares to what I saw three days ago on the bloody battlefields of Antietam. So many men and boys died. We worked hard all day to take the wounded from the field on stretchers so that the doctors could try to save their lives. The surgeons worked without stopping at great risk to themselves. There was no time to think. No time to feel the pain of all the losses. I moved numbly from soldier to soldier doing what I could to help. I didn't mind, though, for I knew I couldn't handle the sorrow that was welling up inside me.

Our nearest hospital was within range of enemy shells, but we had five other camp hospitals nearby. We carried stretcher after stretcher of wounded men to waiting ambulances. Generals and privates lay side by side, as death is no respecter of rank. I washed their wounds and gave them water to drink while they waited.

Over and over again, dying men lifted their voices in agony. When I could, I asked each man if he knew the Savior, and while I gave him water from a canteen, I prayed over him and shared a Bible verse or two. The idea that any of these young men could die this day without knowing Jesus as their Redeemer spurred me on.

In this way, I spent the day and the evening. That night, I passed by a pale, sweet face of a young soldier who was severely wounded. The boy grew faint from the loss of blood. I stooped down and asked if there was anything I could do for him. The soldier looked at me with clear, intelligent eyes and said, "Yes, yes. There is something to be done, and quickly for I am dying."

I left the boy and ran to one of the surgeons. He came back with me, examined him, and agreed that this soldier would not live to see the sun rise. I gave the boy some water from my canteen. The boy motioned me closer with a trembling hand. I knelt down beside him and listened with breathless attention to catch the words that fell from his dying lips.

"I am not what I seem. I am a female. I enlisted from the purest motives and have remained undiscovered and unsuspected. I have no mother or father. My only brother was killed today. I closed his eyes an hour before I was wounded. I shall soon be with him for I am a Christian. My trust is in God, and I will die in peace, but I wish you to bury me with your own hands that none may know after my death that I am a girl. I know I can trust you."

I spoke gently to her. "Yes, I will do what you ask." I found a chaplain, and we prayed with her. I stayed with her until she died about an hour later, and then I got help from a fellow soldier to dig her grave, but I alone laid her down in the grave so no one but I would know her secret. I found a spot under a mulberry tree where, in another time, the sounds of birds, not cannons will be heard. Her sorrows are now over and her race is won. She's found the heavenly shore and touched the face of God.

Mollie, this girl's death affected me more than any other death I have witnessed in this war. As I knelt by her grave, tucked under a tree on a hill overlooking a field where so many died, tears poured down my face. I cried for her. I cried for this country. I cried for myself. This girl could just as easily have been me. I don't know why God has spared my life so far, but may I serve him with all my heart and soul just as this young girl did.

No sooner had I buried this precious girl than I came upon the unconscious, wounded body of James. I screamed out, "No! It cannot be!" As I bent over him, my tears fell on his face. I poured water from my canteen gently on his head. He was severely wounded and barely breathing. Even the cool water did not rouse him. We quickly moved him to a field hospital where he waited for surgery.

I tended his wounds as best I could, but he needed help, more help than he could get here in this makeshift hospital. Most of the wounded are now moved to Frederick, where homes, churches, and shops are turned into hospitals. But I wanted to get James to the city—to a general hospital. I greatly feared for his life. I begged leave to take James myself. Some of the ambulance trains go to Baltimore, some to Philadelphia, and some to Washington. The closest general hospital is in Baltimore, and I was given a pass to take James there. Days passed until I could get an empty berth. The trains are filled with broken men.

Finally, today we took an ambulance train to Baltimore. I took fresh straw to make a bed for him on the train, which was crowded with the wounded. The train swayed and shook. I could see the bursts of pain in James's eyes as he struggled to steady himself with each turn. I held him so that he would not feel the startling jerking of the train, but his wounds are deep. I prayed with each rattle of the train car that he would make it to Baltimore alive. The young soldier to my right died right after the trip began and several more in our car failed to make it to the city.

Once we were in Baltimore, I begged help from a passerby to carry James on a stretcher to the closest general hospital. I am by his side now. He finally rests on a makeshift bed, and now the waiting begins. His breathing is labored. I will not leave him. Several times today, he came into consciousness and I told him he would make it. His eyes would flutter and then close again. Hours have passed. He lies so still. I write a page to you and then turn to him to wipe his brow. He has not moved. There is nothing more I can do. Oh, why is there so much death and destruction?

As it neared midnight, James tried to talk. I leaned over to catch his words. The words came in broken phrases. "Frank, there is nothing ... nothing more for me to do ... I have fought ... the good fight ... am ready to go home now ... to my heavenly Father."

"No, James," I urged him. "Your time is not up yet. You have much to teach me. I cannot bear the thought of marching a step without you. You have never failed me yet. You cannot fail me now."

"Frank," he whispered in a strained voice, "you are not alone. You will know the way. You'll see." And then he was gone.

I have wept until there are no more tears. The tears threaten to wash away all I have written to you. This cruel war. It takes the finest of them all and leaves the rest of us to grieve. I cannot bear the sadness, Mollie.

Your friend,

Emma

Fort McHenry, Baltimore

September 22, 1862

Dear Emma,

Four days of surgeries. I spend days and nights in the hospital ward and catch sleep as I can on a cot. The wounded poured in to our ward. Cots are set up on the grounds as well. The Confederate doctors, all political prisoners, offered their services which were quickly accepted by Dr. Bruden. Federal and Confederate doctors alike work on Federal and Confederate soldiers. No one stops to ask which side the man fought for. The goal is the same—to save a life.

Old Jim, the peddler, came by tonight when I returned to my cell. He told me he helped out too on the grounds of the fort, moving the wounded from stretchers to makeshift cots. "Aye, I stared into the face of each one of them blue boys—gonna find the soldier who betrayed me, I am. One day." His bitterness consumes him and I had no time for his tirades tonight. I called the guard to get Old Jim to move on.

This is worse than anything I ever saw at Robertson Hospital. The wounded are mangled and bleeding. There are not enough bandages or medicine. The sounds, Emma, are the worst. The sounds of men in horrible pain. I search each face and say a prayer of thanks when I realize it is not you I am seeing. I pray you are safe.

I'm under orders to rest tomorrow and get some sleep. I don't know how I shall when so much needs to be done, but Dr. Bruden won't let me back into the hospital ward until I do. I best follow his orders. I think there will be weeks of surgeries and care for the wounded. Mr. Stone just came by with some more writing paper, his secret ink powder, and a piece of candy. I looked surprised, and he said, "Proud of you, Mollie. Now get some rest."

Your friend,

Mollie

Fort McHenry, Baltimore

September 23, 1862

Dear Mollie,

I've cried all the tears I dare shed. I must do what James would want me to do. There are many wounded here and my services are needed. I reported to the Provost General to get new orders. I could return to the field hospital with my unit or stay here in Baltimore to work at a general hospital for awhile. There will not be fighting again anytime soon. Both sides must recover from that bloody day at Antietam.

The Provost General has ordered me to Fort McHenry to help out there. It seems the wounded that cannot be tended to in the city hospitals are being sent to Fort McHenry. I enjoyed a nice walk from the city to the harbor and took a boat over to the fort from there. I wish I had time to visit your great aunt, but she's probably not returned from Richmond. Your last letter to reach me told me about your successful mission and your expected trip the next day. I haven't heard anything from you since, but with all this fighting, I'm sure it'll take some time for your letters to catch up with me.

I reported in at the fort and was assigned temporary quarters. I was assigned to the hospital ward where I served all day. It's good to be nursing again. The Confederate doctors are skilled. The Federal surgeons work well with them. It's also good to work with those who do not care about the color of the uniform. If only we could work together and not care about the color of the skin.

Your friend,

Emma

Fort McHenry, Baltimore

September 24, 1862

Dear Emma,

I have to admit that the rest did me good. Dr. Bruden had a long list of assignments for me when I reported to the ward, and I spent much of my time scrubbing the surgical tools—a gruesome task but one Captain Sally would have applauded. Finally, in the afternoon, I was back by the bedside of the men, which is much preferred to being elbow deep in soapsuds.

I changed the bandage of a young Federal soldier and talked to him of home. His thoughts of his mother and sister waiting for him gave him strength. I wondered about my mother and sister. I hope the letter I gave to Dr. Stone was successfully smuggled out. I don't want them to worry about me.

Dr. Bruden barked instructions for a medicinal paste to a Federal soldier, a nurse. He hurried away to make the concoction. The person looked familiar, but from across the ward I couldn't make out who it was. I gathered up the soiled bandages and put them in a basket.

Dr. Bruden signaled for me to assist him. I began to wash out the wound as Dr. Bruden looked on. He examined the patient's wound and then asked me to get a certain medicine from the dispensery. When I turned the corner into the room, I couldn't believe my eyes. There you were, standing there, in the blue uniform of the North!

When Dr. Bruden shouted for me to hurry with the medicine, I was so flustered that I fumbled around in the cabinets trying to find it. I was so relieved when you found the right medicine vial and handed it to me. You must have been just as shocked as I was.

The next two hours were torture. We both had so much to say to each other and yet our paths did not cross again. The guard came to take me back to my cell, and I didn't want to go. I was

hoping we'd have a few moments to tell you about what landed me here. I'm a political prisoner — a Rebel spy. I have no idea how long I will be here.

Tomorrow, I hope you shall have this letter. I have used almost all of my secret ink to tell you everything. Now if only I can get it to you.

Until we meet again,

Mollie

Fort McHenry, Baltimore

SEPTEMBER 25, 1862

Dear Mollie,

In the morning, I was assigned to help on the fort grounds and not able to get back to the ward. It was so difficult to focus on my duties, knowing you were probably in that hospital ward. I had to see you again.

I told the Federal surgeon that more bandages were needed. He sent someone else to fetch them. An hour later, I told him that more quinine was needed. Once again he sent someone else. The many wounded needed every skilled nurse and doctor available, and he was not going to spare me that day. You must have felt the frustration too. I wondered if you were looking for me in the ward.

What a fortunate turn of events when you came out to the grounds today. I had to smile as you marched right up to the surgeon in charge and said you were there to collect the surgeon's tools for scrubbing. My heart sank when he replied that he could not release his tools until nightfall. Would I not be able to see you again? How cool and calm you sounded when you said there were freshly scrubbed tools for him, but you couldn't carry anything that could be used as a weapon. I held my breath. Was this going to be my chance?

And thank God, it was. Without your quick thinking, I could never have so readily volunteered to go with you. If he'd known who you were really with, I'd never have this packet of letters that you slipped to me as we walked back to the hospital ward.

It was three more hours before I was relieved of my duties and able to find a place alone to read your letters. In the last envelope you gave me some of the special ink powder of Mr. Stone. I am indebted to a Confederate for the ability to write to you now!

Mollie, I have to get you out of here. I don't know if you know this, but President Lincoln has suspended the writ of habeas corpus.

That means that for the duration of the war, political prisoners can be held indefinitely without a trial. You will likely be here for the rest of the war, if I don't figure a way to get you out. For now, let's pass notes to each other while I work on a plan. It is so good to see you, Mollie. You are quite the nurse … and the spy!

Your friend,

Emma

Fort McHenry, Baltimore

September 27, 1862

Dear Emma,

For two days now you've been assigned to the temporary ward on the grounds and I to the hospital ward. Our paths haven't crossed at all. Tonight is my French lesson. Mr. Stone tells me it is moved to the strategy room because the doctors who usually teach the lesson are worn out and need their rest. I'll have more movement than usual. I hope I will see you.

The peddler just came by again and stared at me. "Who are you writing to, pretty Rebel spy?" I replied it was just notes in my journal and turned away from him. He continued to stare for several minutes before he shuffled off down the hall. I do not like that man.

The guard and Mr. Stone came by for me at seven o'clock. Mr. Stone gave me some more paper and ink. "For your lessons," he said, but we both knew it was more than enough for one night's lesson. When I got to the lesson, I began to straighten the sheets of paper. I gasped. Mr. Stone kicked me under my desk. I looked at him in surprise, and he nodded and smiled. It was a letter tucked under the writing paper. From Momma and Sissy! Mr. Stone's daughter managed to smuggle my letter out of prison and to a trusted mail carrier. My letter made it all the way to Richmond and Momma's back to me! Oh thank you, Mr. Stone! I hugged the papers close to my chest and the French lesson could not go fast enough. I could not wait to get back to my cell to read the letter.

After the class, the guard escorted me and Mr. Stone back to our cells. I asked where the Federal soldiers stay, and the guard told me it was none of my business. I was sorry I couldn't see you tonight, but the letter from Momma was read ten times over! I have to get home to my family. Can you help me?

Your friend,

Mollie

Fort McHenry, Baltimore

OCTOBER 2, 1862

Dear Mollie,

I have a plan. I've been given orders to return to my unit and must leave soon to catch up with my unit at Harper's Ferry. At least we were both assigned to the hospital ward these last few days. I'm sure you were as frustrated as I was that there was no time to speak alone. But at least we were together, and it has given me some time to watch how they treat you and when the guard is paying attention to you. It seems that as long as you move in and out among the hospital beds, he tends to ignore you. It's only when you accompany him to and from the ward or to other rooms that he vigilantly watches you. We'll take advantage of this tomorrow. Watch for my cue and be ready for anything.

Your friend,

Emma

Richmond, Virginia

OCTOBER 10, 1862

Dear Emma,

Be ready for anything? Well, my good friend, that was good advice! The next day I was working in the hospital ward with Dr. Bruden barking orders as usual. You were nowhere to be seen. I supposed you were assigned to the temporary ward on the grounds again. At midday, the doctors took a break to eat. Several more men died that morning and were waiting transport to the morgue. An orderly moved their bodies to the stretchers on the floor. I was to make up their beds. I went to the cupboard and gathered fresh linens.

I got to the third bed, whipped off the blanket, and began to strip the bed. That's when I saw it. A uniform of a federal soldier—tattered, but neatly folded. I looked around but didn't see you anywhere. I looked at the guard. He was talking with another guard. I pulled the uniform into my basket of soiled linens, covered it up, and quickly remade the bed. I continued on, remaking the beds. My hands worked quickly, stripping soiled linens and smartly making up the clean sheets on each bed, but my mind was spinning. A disguise. I knew it was from you. But what was your plan?

I stepped over the dead bodies lined up on the stretchers and carried the basket of soiled linens to the wash buckets in the closet and began to scrub them. The swishing sounds of the scrub brush kept the guard's attention on his conversation with his friend. He knew his charge was hard at work.

When I was sure he was no longer checking on me, I quickly put on the uniform I pulled my long hair up on top of my head and wound it around and tucked it under the blue Federal cap. I came in wearing the gray cloth of the Confederates; it's only fair to leave wearing the blue of the Federals. I shoved my dress under the huge piles of soiled linens. It would take days of scrubbing before anyone

found it. But now what? You were still nowhere to be found. I kept scrubbing the wash and prayed the guard would not come check on me now.

Suddenly, I heard a great commotion as you pushed the door open to the ward and called out to my guard that he was needed to help you transport the dead bodies to the morgue. You must have known I was nearby for I heard you say to my guard, "You know, sometimes a body looks so still it seems like it is dead even when it is not."

That's when I knew what you wanted me to do. I crawled around the corner and lay down on an empty stretcher. I tried to breathe as shallowly as I could. I couldn't see a thing with my eyes closed. I heard your voice and that of my guard's coming closer. It was all I could do not to call out when you lifted the stretcher in the air. My heart raced! Where were you taking me? Would the guard look at my face and recognize me? I wished I had pulled my cap down over my forehead. I held my breath. You did a great job of trying to distract him so he wouldn't look down. Soon I heard the sound of gravel crunching under boots, and the warmth of the sun on my face, and I knew we were on the main grounds.

I heard you speak. "There is no more serious duty than carrying the body of a fallen soldier. This one here was my comrade. I need some time alone to say good-bye. Would you mind giving me a few moments?" I felt myself being lowered to the ground. What was happening? Was the guard staring at me? Would he know who I really was?

I could feel my heart pounding when you knelt down by me, on one knee, and began to pray. "Dear Lord, thank you for this fallen comrade. Thank you for the commitment he gave to our cause. Go now with him on this journey to the other side. Bless him, dear Lord, and guide him now home. Amen." I heard the guard grunt and start to walk away. Where was he? Was it safe to open my eyes?

A few minutes later, I held my breath as you gave me your hand and helped me up. We were in the shadow of the walkway. No one

noticed that one soldier knelt down, but two soldiers stood up. You kicked the stretcher behind a post. Then we started to walk across the grounds. "What now?" I whispered.

That's when we rounded the corner and you came face to face with the peddler. My skin crawed when he stared at you with such hatred and hissed, "It's you!" He was so focused on you, I don't think he noticed me.

When Old Jim lunged at you and the two of you fought, my heart nearly stopped. We were in sight of the gate to the fort. We had to get there now—and fast. I was worried the commotion would bring other soldiers and we'd be found out. It only got worse, when Old Jim bumped into me and a piece of my hair fell from under my cap. That's when he recognized me and started shouting, "Rebel spy escaping!" I panicked. A nearby soldier, thinking you were capturing the escaped Rebel spy, jumped in the fray, and you should have heard my heart thudding. I knew you'd have to turn me in, or you too would be imprisoned. I feared the worst as you called out to the soldier, "Grab him. He's an escaped prisoner."

Him? I thought. I'd forgotten that I was disguised as a fellow soldier in Federal blues. I was on your side and the side of this helpful soldier. When he whacked Old Jim on the head and knocked him out, I quickly stuffed the strand of hair back up under my cap. I tried not to laugh as you praised the young soldier and had him haul Old Jim away to a cell for interrogation.

My heart started racing again when you pushed me into a nearby horse cart, covered me with a tarp, and flicked the reins. I held my breath when I heard the guard ask for your pass. I tried not to move a muscle when you flipped open the other side of the tarp and showed the guard bags of mail. I knew your credentials still list you as regimental postmaster of the 2nd Michigan Volunteer Infantry, but what would you say if the guard discovered me? You were so cool. I heard you whistle as you clucked for the horse to walk on past the guardhouse. I wished you had raced her out of there, but you weren't going to give us away. It wasn't until we were

through the gate and a long ways down the road that I felt safe enough to come out from under the tarp.

Oh, how I was thrilled to see the Baltimore train station. Thankfully, there was so much activity there that two more Federal officers, both with tickets, but only one with papers, were not noticed. I needed the train ride back to Washington to settle down. We couldn't say much on the train, but I was silently thanking God for your quick thinking, your courage, and your friendship. You risked your life for me, and I will never forget it.

After our adventure together, it was hard to part in Washington. Thank you for arranging my passage to Richmond with our mail carrier who has so faithfully delivered our letters for many months. I learned while at Fort McHenry that a number of men were imprisoned there for just the same thing. Our carrier was willing to risk his safety to see me back to Richmond, and it felt good to be in the company of someone we knew and trusted.

Now you are back with your unit and more service to the Federal government. And I am back with Momma and Sissy and Great Auntie. Imagine their surprise when I returned. They had kept busy the same way I had—nursing soldiers. The number of wounded from the Second Battle of Manassas had Momma daily at Robertson Hospital. Even Great Auntie nurses the Confederate soldiers with as much energy as if they were Federals. They were busy, but worried. When my letter came through the lines, they felt much better, though they were troubled as to when I would be released. Momma said, "Imagine, Mollie, they thought you were a spy!"

The Richmond kin are quite proud of Great Auntie for her smuggling of contraband across Federal lines. They no longer gossip about her behind her back, especially when they saw she was able to safely smuggle out such a lovely hat! Once I was back home, Great Auntie placed the hat on my head for all to admire. I had to admire her spunk and wondered how she was able to hide the hat from the searchers on the flag-of-truce boat. She winked at me

and said that an old lady's billowing skirts can sometimes come in handy.

I wanted to go see Miss Van Lew and tell her all about my adventures, but it's not safe. Especially now, I must be very careful. I would never want to endanger her network. One day. Perhaps. But for now, wars are for secrets.

And now, my dear, good friend. You have faithfully tended the wounded and dying for so long and carried out all of your duties with courage and grace. You move from person to person, duty to duty, in the midst of danger without any thought of your own safety. Your faith in God has not wavered amidst the horrors of what man can do to man. You have trusted him each day with your life and led so many others to know his love. And you were willing to risk your freedom for mine.

You have longed for all to know freedom. For the slave, you have desired freedom of body, mind, and spirit—no longer in bondage to any man. For everyone you meet, you have desired freedom of salvation that comes from Jesus Christ alone. You have labored well.

Charlie just came by with word that while I was gone, President Lincoln announced his Emancipation Proclamation. In just a few months, on the first of January, all slaves everywhere will be free. Now we must continue to fight your way and mine—to make sure that it is the Union that prevails. Then we shall have a glorious reunion.

You, dear Emma, are a remarkable lady. There will come a day when you lay down the blue uniform and willingly take up your skirts again. When that day comes, I will contribute to your outfit its crowning glory. You, my friend, shall have my contraband hat!

Your friend forever,

Mollie

Epilogue

By the time of the Emancipation Proclamation, the war was not even half over. Much more hardship, grief, and loss would come to both the North and the South. This "great war" often required people on both sides of the many issues that divided our country to decide for themselves what they believed and what they would be willing to sacrifice for those beliefs.

Elizabeth Van Lew

Elizabeth Van Lew developed her own carefully guarded code and sent important information to Union generals through trusted individuals. Ordinary people such as store clerks, shoemakers, servants, bakers, delivery persons, and seamstresses formed her secret network. Mary Elizabeth Bowser, once a Van Lew slave, was one of the most unusually placed spies in the Van Lew spy network. Educated by the Van Lews in Philadelphia, Mary Elizabeth Bowser relied on her photographic memory and her position as a maid in the home of Confederate President Jefferson Davis to secure important information for the Union.

False bottom trays, hollowed-out soles of shoes, books, eggs, or seamstress's patterns hid many secrets for those in the Van Lew network. Miss Van Lew's "Crazy Bet" persona served brilliantly to provide her the cover she needed for her secret activities and helped her avoid detection throughout the entire war. At the end of the war, General Ulysses S. Grant said, "You have sent me the most valuable information received from Richmond during the war." When he became president of the United States, he designated her Postmaster of Richmond, a position she held for his two terms as president.

However, many in Richmond despised Miss Van Lew as a traitor to the Southern cause. She lived a very lonely life and died nearly penniless in 1900. Relatives of some of the former Libby prisoners she had helped, including those of the great-grandson of the Revolutionary patriot Paul Revere, raised money for the stone they sent from Boston to mark her grave. On the stone, they inscribed these words:

She risked everything that is dear to man—
friends, fortune, comfort, health, life itself,
all for one absorbing desire of her heart—
that slavery might be abolished and the Union preserved.

Captain Sally Tompkins

During the Civil War, Sally Tompkins nursed 1,333 Confederate soldiers in her 22-bed Robertson Hospital at the corner of Third and Main Streets in Richmond, Virginia, with the remarkable record of returning 94 percent of them to service. Threatened with the Confederate government's decision to close all private hospitals, Sally Tompkins presented Confederate President Jefferson Davis with the evidence of the success of her hospital. Impressed with her record, President Davis commissioned Sally Tompkins as a captain in the Confederate Cavalry, making Robertson Hospital an official government hospital. Captain Sally became the only female officer of the Civil War—Confederate or Union.

A stickler for cleanliness, Sally Tompkins was said to have ruled her hospital with a stick in one hand and a Bible in the other. Captain Sally held nightly prayer meetings and, if a soldier was to sick too attend, Captain Sally would come by his bed later that night to pray with him and read the Bible to him. Whenever Captain Sally discharged a patient, she sent him off with a knapsack packed with a blanket, clean clothes, warm socks she knitted herself, and a copy of the Gospels bound in oil cloth.

The Cary Cousins

Constance Cary and her two cousins Hetty and Jennie sewed the first flags of the Confederacy in September 1861 and delivered them to Generals Johnson, Beuregard, and Van Dorn to be carried into battle. In 1865, Hetty Cary married John Pegram, a dashing brigadier general in the Confederacy, and son of Mrs. Pegram, who ran the well-known school for girls. Just three weeks later, he was killed in battle. After the war, Constance Cary married Burton Harrison, an aid to President Jefferson Davis, moved to New York City, and became a writer.

Great Uncle Chester and Great Aunt Belle

After the war, Great Uncle Chester resumed his medical practice in Washington, and found his greatest pleasure in teaching medical students and in urging a greater acceptance of women at medical schools. Great Aunt Belle, thrilled to be home again, invited Mollie to live with them to finish her studies (paid for with United States dollars).

Sissy and Lemuel

After four years in the Confederate cavalry, Lem was so comfortable in the saddle, he and Sissy bought a small farm in the country and raised a family of four children, all boys. Sissy was glad she had learned to sew shirts. She still couldn't knit very well but Aunt Mollie came through with plenty of socks for her nephews.

Charlie

The day he turned sixteen, Charlie enlisted in the Confederate army. Having practiced the drummer's calls on Mollie's veranda so often, Charlie was a smashing success. Molly saved all the newspapers for Charlie while he was gone.

Mollie Turner

Mollie continued her work as a member of Miss Van Lew's spy ring throughout the war. It became more dangerous to speak to Miss Van Lew during the last part of the war, so Mollie's contacts were limited mostly to the Simpsons at their store. But occasionally, Mollie received a letter from Adam Evers that she warmed in the oven and that led to more exciting adventures. Mr. Evers finished medical school at Johns Hopkins, and after the war, having been introduced by Mollie to Great Uncle Chester, he joined him in his practice in Washington. There, the Greats were pleased to keep a watchful eye on a budding romance between the young doctor and their great niece who had come to live with them.

Emma Edmonds a/k/a Private Franklin Thompson

Emma Edmonds continued as Private Franklin Thompson with the 2nd Michigan Volunteer Infantry, and there is much more to her story than could be told here. In 1863, when Emma became ill with malaria, the doctors required Private Thompson to be hospitalized. Emma had a tough decision to make. Stay and hope she would not be examined and her secret discovered, or desert the army? In the spring of 1863, Private Frank Thompson disappeared from the ranks of Company F of the 2nd Michigan.

While recovering from her illness, Frank became Emma once again. During this time, she wrote *Nurse and Spy in the Union Army.* Not ready yet to reveal the connection between herself and Frank Thompson, she used initials and changed some details to obscure the identity of the main character. Mr. Hurlburt, her previous employer, published *Nurse and Spy,* which Emma dedicated to the sick and wounded soldiers of the Army of the Potomac. It was an overnight bestseller, selling hundreds of thousands of copies. Emma donated the proceeds of the book to the Christian Commission and to veterans' aid organizations.

In 1864, with the Civil War still raging, and many wounded soldiers still in need of care, Emma joined the Christian Commission and worked at a hospital in Harper's Ferry, West Virginia. In 1867, she married Linus Seelye, and together they raised a family, finally settling in Texas.

Years later, in 1882, Emma contacted members of Company F of the 2nd Michigan Infantry who had served with her, surprising her fellow soldiers with the true story of "Frank Thompson." Emma sought their assistance to secure a government pension for her years of military service. Her fellow soldiers submitted numerous affidavits[1] to Congress that attested to her faithful service as soldier and nurse in the Union army. The many affirmations may best be summed up by the captain who mustered her into Company F of the 2nd Michigan in the first place:

---

[1] House Report No. 820 to accompany H.R. 5334, u.s. Congress, March 18, 1884

"S. Emma E. Seelye, by her uniform faithfulness, bravery, and efficiency, and by her pure morals and Christian character, won the respect, admiration, and confidence of both officers and men in said company and regiment." — Captain William Morse

In 1884, the United States Congress granted Emma her soldier's pension, stating that the fact that "Franklin Thompson and Mrs. Sarah E. E. Seelye are one and the same person is established by abundance of proof and beyond a doubt." In 1897, Emma became the only woman to be mustered into the Grand Army of the Republic as a regular member, and in 1988 she was inducted into the Military Intelligence Hall of Fame.

As Emma concluded her own story in *Nurse and Spy*, she expressed the passion of her heart:

And now I lay aside my pen, hoping that after "this cruel war is over" and peace shall have once more shed her sweet influence over our land, I may be permitted to resume it again to record the annihilation of rebellion, and the final triumph of Truth, Right, and Liberty.

> *O Lord of Peace, who art Lord of Righteousness,*
> *Constrain the anguished worlds from sin and grief*
> *Pierce them with conscience, purge them with redress*
> *And give us peace, which is no counterfeit!*

Now the Lord is Spirit; and where the spirit of the Lord is, there is liberty.
2 Corinthians 3:17

Dear Reader,

When I wrote Liberty Letters, I intended to communicate America's journey of freedom and also illustrate the personal faith journey of girls who made bold choices to help others and in doing so, helped shape the course of history. Through their stories, we learn the facts, customs, lifestyles of days gone by, and so much more.

The girls I wrote about didn't consider themselves part of "history." Few people do. These were ordinary girls going about their lives when challenging times occurred in the communities in which they lived. They discovered integrity, courage, hope, and faith within themselves as they met these challenges with creativity and imagination. American history is steeped with just these kinds of people. These people embody liberty.

At least 400, and maybe as many as 1,000 disguised women were soldiers in the Civil War. Emma Edmonds, a private in the Union Army, was one of those women. Not only do military records confirm her service, but she left us with her own story, *Nurse and a Spy in the Union Army*, first published in 1864. No one suspected she wrote about herself at the time, however, because the idea that a woman would serve in the military was pure fiction!

Yet twenty years later, Emma's military pension file, the Congressional record, sworn affidavits of fellow soldiers and officers, and Emma's official statement provided proof that the United States government needed to declare that Emma Edmonds Seelye and Private Franklin Thompson of Company F of the 2nd Michigan Infantry were one in the same.

I wanted to tell Emma's story and explore the motivation behind her commitment. After all, Emma could have served as a civilian nurse—as she did with the Christian Commission of West Virginia when she reclaimed her female identity. To tell Emma's story, I adapted some of Emma's adventures in *Nurse and a Spy*. I often kept her words as close to her own voice as possible, especially where she shared her personal Christian faith and beliefs.

Did Emma have a friend like Mollie during the war? As far as we know, Emma kept her identity a closely guarded secret. With the exception of one fellow soldier, it is likely that no one knew her secret at the time. But as an author, I wondered what it would have been like if Emma had shared her secret—and her adventures—with a good friend like Mollie Turner. That part of the story is fiction. Yet, one can imagine the need Emma had to share her real self with someone. Perhaps that is why she so quickly wrote her story after leaving the army—she just had to tell someone about her adventures, even if no one knew it was she who had them!

Your friend,

Nancy LeSourd

Emma Edmonds,
circa 1860–1861, in male civilian dress

" ... I had no other motive in enlisting than love to God and love for suffering humanity. I felt called to go and do what I could for the defense of the right ..."

Report 820 to accompany H.R. 5334, United States Congress, March 18, 1884, Franklin Thompson, Alias, S.E.E. Seelye, Statement of S. Emma E. Seelye

Union Solider's Canteen,
circa 1861–65

Copy of *Nurse and Spy in the Union Army: The Adventures and Experiences of a Woman in Hospitals, Camps, and Battle Fields* by S. Emma E. Edmonds, 1864

Post Office at Headquarters, Army of the Potomac

Receiving letters from home was an important part of the soldier's life, whether he fought for the Union or the Confederacy.

Cross Carved by
Unknown Soldier
of the 77th NY Vol.
Infantry

Wounded Soldiers in Hospital, circa 1861–1865

Elizabeth Van Lew, circa 1864

Van Lew Mansion, circa 1906

Elizabeth Van Lew's Cipher Code

Van Lew relied on a cipher code, hidden in her watch case, and a colorless liquid to create her dispatches to Union generals. The code appeared when milk was applied to the message.

"LIBBY PRISON."
THE ONLY PICTURE IN EXISTENCE.
AS IT APPEARED
AUGUST 23. 1863

Libby Prison, 1863

Sally Tompkins

Sally Tompkins nursed 1,333 Confederate soldiers in her 22-bed Robertson Hospital in Richmond with the remarkable record of only 73 deaths over a four-year period. Captain Sally sent off her recovered patient with a knapsack packed with a blanket, clean clothes, warm socks she often knitted herself, and a copy of the Gospels bound in oil cloth.

In the Hospital, 1861
By William Ludwell Sheppard

One soldier's unraveled tent became another soldier's knitted socks at the hands of Mary Greenhow Lee, sister-in-law of Confederate spy Rose Greenhow.

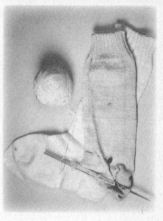

Negative by J. Gardner Positive by A. Gardner
HEADQUARTERS CHRISTIAN COMMISSION, IN THE FIELD, GERMANTOWN, SEPTEMBER, 1863   *PLATE 33*

Christian Commission in the Field

**Property of
Pvt. Stephen H. Leonard,
Company A, 3ʳᵈ Company,
Massachusetts Volunteer
Cavalry**, sent to his parents
after his death in action in 1864.
Among other items, his property
included a wallet, toothbrush,
patriotic bookmark, a diary,
comb, and a button bag.

Alexander Gardner, 1862

President Lincoln and General George B. McClellan

General's tent after the Battle of Antietam, October 3, 1862

Courtesy, National Archives

Emancipation Proclamation, January 1, 1863

Young Soldier, 1861

by Winslow Homer

Liberty Letters

Attack at Pearl Harbor

Nancy LeSourd

kidz

Somewhere Over the Pacific Ocean

OCTOBER 25, 1940

Dear Catherine,

Mother always says my big mouth gets me into trouble. But today it got me into the cockpit of a Clipper Ship!

Granddaddy insisted we take the Pan Am Clipper for the last part of our trip from San Francisco to Pearl Harbor. When Mother said it was too expensive, he said we'll use military vehicles for the rest of our lives. He wanted us to have this once-in-a-lifetime experience.

But that's just it. If this is the only time I'm on a flying airship, I've got to truly experience it. That's where an eight-year-old brother who can't sit still comes in handy. I told Mother I'd watch Gordon while he went to explore. Mother leaned back, closed her eyes, and murmured, "Uh huh," which I took to mean yes.

Gordo has no clue how lucky we are to fly on a Clipper Ship. This flying ship can land on water, has places for us to sleep, and makes it possible to cross oceans in days instead of weeks. Gordo wanted to find out if a celebrity was in the deluxe cabin, but I was tired of the passenger deck. We'd already spent a lot of time here. I tugged at my dress, which had wrinkled dreadfully. I'd have to change for dinner, for sure. We've eaten all our meals in the elegant dining room with its starched white tablecloths, gleaming china and crystal, and sterling silverware. Mother insisted we dress to match. I think it's stupid to wear my white gloves to dinner, just to take them off, and try not to get any food on them.

As we walked along the passenger deck, we kept bumping into stewards wanting to fulfill my every need. "Juice, Miss Lyons?" "Another blanket, Miss Lyons?" "Care for tea, Miss Lyons?" Very annoying. What I wanted to see was the cockpit, but I didn't dare ask the steward for that. After poking around the deluxe cabin and finding no sign of a Hollywood star, Gordo was finally willing to go upstairs to the crew deck.

A small sign said "Personnel Only," but I pretended I didn't see it. While the stewards were busy, we crept up the staircase. Gordo was drawn to chocolate chip cookie smells coming from the kitchen (they call it a galley), but I pulled him on down the hall. We inched past a room where a crew member sorted mail into three different mailbags Gordo's size. The door next to the mail room flung open. We hid in its shadow as a uniformed man with papers folded under his arm marched down the hall. The sign on the door said "Navigation."

"He's headed to the cockpit," I whispered. "Let's follow him."

"Are you crazy?" Gordo said. "They're gonna kick us out of here."

"Thousands of feet above the Pacific Ocean? I don't think so. But if you're scared, go back downstairs to Mother."

Gordo shook his head, but stayed behind me as I walked toward the cockpit. We slipped by the mail room and the kitchen. The cook sang at the top of his lungs while he banged pots and pans. Gordo started giggling. I elbowed him hard, for we were right outside the cockpit door. I heard voices inside that door. "What ya gonna do now?" whispered Gordo.

The door handle turned, and I held my breath. A uniformed man stepped out of the cockpit. "Well, well, what do we have here?"

Gordo shrank back behind me. I put out my gloved hand. "Hello, sir, I'm Meredith Lyons."

"Pleased to meet you, Miss Lyons, and you too, young Master Lyons, I assume?" Gordo nodded. "Hmm ... A bit off course, are you? The stairs to the passenger deck are right over there."

Gordo started toward the stairs, and I yanked him back. "Sir, I wondered if we could see the cockpit? We've never been on an airship before."

"Not really allowed, young lady, but I'll check with the captain." He disappeared back into the cockpit. A few minutes later, he cracked the door and said, "Sorry, but you'll have to return to the passenger deck."

I stepped forward and put my foot right inside the door so that the officer couldn't shut it. He looked annoyed, but I was

determined to get inside. "Sir, you see, my whole life I've wanted to see inside a cockpit. I keep a scrapbook of all these articles about flying and planes and Amelia Earhart and everything. Sir, did you know, not too long ago, she took a photograph of a Clipper flying to California while she was flying her plane to Honolulu? Isn't that something! This might even be the exact same plane Amelia Earhart took a picture of! Everyone's been so nice down below, but it's what you important men do up here that really interests me. Please, sir. Won't you ask one more time?"

Gordo looked like he was going to die and begged me to leave before the man came back. I told him, "No way."

It seemed like an hour, but finally the officer opened the door, and said, "After you, Miss Lyons." I pushed by Gordo to get inside before the officer changed his mind.

The captain checked the dials and instruments in front of him. The other pilot scribbled something in a large brown logbook. Numbers, I think. The navigator scooted over and let Gordo sit next to him. The copilot stood up, and pointing to his seat, said, "Miss Lyons?"

As I slipped into the seat, I stared at the vast expanse of sky before me. The stars lit up the inky darkness surrounding the plane. After a few minutes, the copilot asked me what I thought. I blinked hard. The stars were still there. Without taking my eyes off the window, I whispered, "Thank you."

Back downstairs in our seats, Gordo went on and on about what he'd seen in the cockpit. Mother was furious at me. "Young lady, your father and I try to teach you what's right and proper, but you constantly amaze me. How dare you bother those pilots while they're doing their job? You know better. And to get Gordon caught up in your scheme too. Won't you ever learn?" I stared out the window and tried to block it all out. This wasn't a good time to bring up my wanting to learn to fly again. I heard Mother's voice in my head. "Absolutely not. It's simply not an option." We'd been through this a million times before over the last few years.

No, not even today on my birthday would this be a good topic of conversation.

I apologized to Mother for bothering the pilots, being a bad example for Gordo, embarrassing her, and not conducting myself as the daughter of a Naval officer. I said all the right things, but inside I was glad I'd done it. I'll never forget turning sixteen. Somehow, some way, before I turn seventeen, I'll find a way to fly.

Maybe this new assignment to Pearl Harbor will be the start of something new. After all, they call Hawaii "paradise," and what would be more heavenly than taking off into the skies, circling the clouds, and landing again—all by myself.

Your high-flying friend,

Merrie

Norfolk, Virginia

NOVEMBER 1, 1940

Dear Merrie,

I've missed you! Norfolk's not the same without you. Guess what? Dad got transfer orders to the Naval Air Station at Kaneohe. We're coming to Hawaii too!

Mom makes lists and posts them everywhere—the bathroom mirror, the refrigerator, the car dashboard. Mom and Dad talk late at night. There's much to do to get Dad ready to go, and with Hank and all, it's a challenge.

When I visited Hank today, Nurse Reynolds told me the Naval Hospital's right on the water. I can picture my brother with a bed next to a large window so he can see the palm trees and feel the warm breezes. It might make up for these horrid six months in the iron lung.

Standing next to Hank's head and talking to him, I try to block out the sounds of the iron prison he's been in for these last six months. Every day I've visited him, I've hated that machine, even though it helps him breathe as it pushes and pulls the air in his chest.

I remember listening to the radio with Hank a few months ago, when Sea Biscuit set that new track record. Hank shouted as loud as he could when the machine would let him speak. Whoosh-whooo. "Go, Biscuit!" Whoosh-whoo. "You can—" Whoosh-whoo "—do it, boy." The announcer said this patched-up crippled horse roared to the finish line in the last stretch of the race. I could see in Hank's eyes that he wants to be just like Biscuit—a down-and-out, "patched-up cripple" who astonishes people with what he can do. Hank's determined to walk again, but his determination breaks my heart. I feel so guilty keeping the truth from him, but I don't have the nerve to tell him what the doctors told us.

You remember what a great baseball player Hank was before he

got polio—especially last year on his seventh-grade team? Boy, could he hit! I'll never forget the crack of the bat as it connected with the ball every time. But now, the only sports he can play are in his head. When Hank listens to games on the radio, he forgets he can't move his legs and pretends he's his old self again. That's just it, though, it's all pretend.

Mom wants me to spend more time with my friends, but I know how much Hank looks forward to my visits. I feel so guilty if I don't come by. When I go to the movies with my friends, I feel like I shouldn't enjoy myself. After all, what fun does Hank have in that iron prison? I tell myself I go to the movies to see the newsreels, to write articles for the school paper. It's like I can't allow myself to just enjoy the movie. Not when Hank's been through so much. I know I'm protective of Hank, but golly, he can't even breathe on his own. Sometimes I hate all this. I wish things were back the way they were—before Hank got sick.

Your friend,

Catherine

Pearl Harbor, Hawaii

NOVEMBER 13, 1940

Dear Catherine,

I can't wait until you get here! I told Mother and Dad right
away. Gordo's announced to one and all that his best friend, Hank,
is coming. Hank's such a good sport to put up with this hero
worship.

I can walk to the tennis courts right next to the hospital. I've
been playing almost every day, but I miss my favorite doubles
partner. Hurry up and get here! I need your help to discourage all
these grown-ups who think I'm going to grow up to be just like
Mother.

You know the drill the first weeks at a new base. Lots of official
visits, shaking hands, and being polite. Last week, when the officers
and their wives visited us, I must have heard ten times, "What a
lovely girl. Is she going to train to be a nurse?"

I cringed as I heard Mother's stock answer, "Our Meredith could
do worse than join us in the medical field or in the Navy."

I faked smiles and shook hands with beautiful officers' wives and
pretended to listen. I did okay until this one woman, Mrs. Eagleton.
She kept pestering me about my nursing plans and asked thousands
of questions. She insisted I come to her house Tuesday night to roll
bandages for the war effort in England. Her daughter, Gwendolyn,
who's my age, will be there. Mother answered for me and said I'd
come. I hate it when she does that.

No, I don't want to be a nurse. And I don't want to be in the
Navy. Unless, of course, they'll let me be a pilot. But no women
can do that now. And roll bandages? That's just more of the same
nursing junk Mother wants me to learn.

Come Tuesday, Mother dropped me off at Mrs. Eagleton's home
with strips of cotton cloth and her best surgical scissors. Mrs.
Eagleton introduced me to everyone as "the daughter of Captain

William J. Lyons, that new surgeon at the hospital, and the lovely Navy nurse, Marilyn Lyons." The women all ooohed and aahhhed. Here it comes, I thought.

"Meredith's going to study to be a nurse too." Inwardly I groaned, but I replied, "Nice to meet you," and took a seat at the dining room table at the farthest end from Mrs. Eagleton, next to the only other girl my age. I plopped my basket of cloth strips on the table.

"I wanted to be a nurse too," Mrs. Eagleton's daughter, Gwendolyn, said. "One day I volunteered at the hospital, but the smells just didn't agree with me."

"It's not for everyone," I replied. Gwendolyn's beautiful. She has long curly red hair and a few perfect freckles across her perfect nose. I stared at her sitting there in her freshly ironed dress. She looked every bit an officer's daughter. Not at all like me. Give me a ponytail and a tennis outfit any day. As Gwendolyn rolled her bandages, I stared at her long slender fingers and painted nails. I curled my fingers to hide the two broken nails from my tennis game.

Mrs. Eagleton jingled a small handbell she kept by her place. An Asian woman, head down, handed fruit punch drinks to everyone. She backed out of the room with her empty tray still held high and gave little nods as she disappeared into the kitchen. Mrs. Eagleton asked, "Has your mother found a maid yet, Meredith? She simply cannot make it here without good help. Not with two children and her duties, you know."

I didn't know. We'd gotten along fine so far, it seemed to me.

"The Jap girls are the best. Why, I've never had a bit of trouble with mine. I check my jewelry after every time she's here. So far, she hasn't taken a thing." Can you believe that pompous old bat said that? Then she said, "I'll get your mother a reference right away. You can't be too careful these days—with the war coming and all."

"Why, I've never had a bit of trouble with mine." So are they some kind of possession? I think not. They're people! They've got names! "You can't be too careful these days." Yeah, like right now. I think I need to be careful who I associate with. Geez, Louise, these

people are opinionated! I sure hope Mother doesn't get a maid. If she does, she'd better not call her "her girl."

Gwendolyn made the night bearable and filled me in on the dances, the boys, and the teachers at Roosevelt High. I started school there the next day. Her boyfriend is a football star. Figures. At the end of the evening, I had stacks of rolled bandages and was exhausted from being nice to Mrs. Eagleton. You'll have to thank me later for going through all this first! Hurry and get here. I need someone normal to talk to.

Your friend,

Mettie

Pearl Harbor, Hawaii

November 17, 1940

Dear Catherine,

School's not so bad here. Lots of Navy kids. Gwendolyn showed me around Roosevelt High the first week. I've never met so many football players. Gwendolyn introduced me to her boyfriend's friends on the team, but they're not my type. I spotted someone who could be though! His name's Drew Masterson. He's in two of my classes, and his father's a pilot with the Army Air Corps. One minor problem: he doesn't know I exist.

Today I went to Waikiki Beach to play volleyball with some kids from school. Gwendolyn watched us play. She didn't want to break a nail. There was another volleyball game going on nearby. When I asked her where those other kids went to school, she said, "Tokyo High."

"What?"

"McKinley High. They've got their school, and we've got ours."

The Japanese thing again. They looked like nice kids to me. I walked over to one of the girls taking a break from her game. "Great serve," I said.

"Thanks!"

"I'm Merrie Lyons. Just moved here from Virginia."

"I'm Janet. Janet Tanaka. Navy or Army?"

"Does it show?"

Janet laughed. "Oahu is overrun with you military kids. Mostly Navy."

"You got it. Navy it is. My parents are at the Naval Hospital. Dad's a doctor; Mother's a nurse."

"Brothers and sisters?" Janet asked.

"One brother. Eight. A real pain."

"Two brothers. Ten and eleven. Definitely a pain."

We talked for half an hour. She's a junior at McKinley High.

Her real name is Miyoko, but she likes her American name, Janet. Her father won't call her anything but Miyoko. He teaches at the Japanese Language School. Miyoko said her parents' generation is worried the kids born in Hawaii will forget all about the ways of Japan and not want to speak Japanese anymore.

"I speak Japanese at home, go by Miyoko, and attend my father's Language School. But as soon as I'm out the door, I'm Janet. Speaking English. Just like this."

Miyoko means "beautiful," and it's a beautiful name. I wish she'd call herself that. But she made it clear, she's "Janet." My friends waved for me to come on. As I went to join them, I realized something. Not once did Miyoko ask me if I was going to be a nurse.

Your friend,

Merrie

Pearl Harbor, Hawaii

November 24, 1940

Dear Catherine,

Get this. There's going to be an aviation course at school next semester! No actual flying, but the instructor's a pilot, and the course covers everything you need to know from the ground. I was the third person to sign up. I checked the sign-up sheet again today. There're twenty-four kids signed up. So far I'm the only girl. I can't wait!

Dad and Mother take us to the Royal Hawaiian Hotel every Saturday afternoon for the tea dances. This week, I saw that boy I like, Drew. He danced the entire time, but not with me. Am I invisible or something? But wow, can he jitterbug!

Gwendolyn was there with her boyfriend, Joe. She made sure all his friends asked me to dance, but I would have traded them all for one dance with Drew. The bands are terrific. Local Hawaiian music mixed right in with Glen Miller and Tommy Dorsey. (Don't you just love "Blueberry Hill"?) The kids here are great dancers. The jitterbug's a slight favorite over the lindy. It's a swell way to meet kids. I'll take you with me the first Saturday you're here.

Gordo wants you to tell Hank "Captain Midnight" is on the radio here too. Here's a note for Hank in secret code. We had to drink gallons of Ovaltine before Gordo collected enough seals to send in for Captain Midnight's Code-O-Graph. Trouble is, Hank has to be able to use his hands, or he won't know what it says. I'll try to find out from Gordo. Right now, he pretends I'm the evil enemy agent and if I get the secret code, all of America will die. Gordo, of course, will save the world since he's the ace aviator, valiant member of Captain Midnight's Secret Squadron (along with every other kid in America!).

I like our Bible class teacher, Jim Downing. He's a gunners mate on the battleship USS *West Virginia* and leads a Bible study on his ship. He's part of a Navigators Bible study in Honolulu too. I told him our fathers were both in a Navigators Bible study back in Norfolk. All the kids like him a lot.

You'll love it here. I'll remind you how to have guilt-free fun again! And you'll be here to keep me out of trouble!

Your friend,

Merrie

Norfolk, Virginia

DECEMBER 2, 1940

Dear Merrie,

I've got the most horrible news. I still can't believe it. Daddy leaves in ten days for Pearl Harbor. Alone! All those late-night discussions Mom and Dad had? Well, they were making decisions all right, but not about what to pack. We're not going with Daddy to Pearl Harbor. And it gets worse. They're sending Hank away to Georgia!

I begged them to change their minds. Daddy says the doctors want to wean Hank off the iron lung, and then Hank can get rehabilitation for his legs. The doctors say the best place for that is Warm Springs Foundation in Georgia.

I do want Hank to get better. You know I do. But he needs us too. I asked Mom if we could move to Warm Springs. Mom said it's not possible. When I asked why not, she and Dad looked funny but didn't say anything. I told them if Hank can't come to Hawaii, then I want Mom and me to go to Georgia. Who else will bring him the sports pages and read to him? Who else will wipe away his tears after the nurses tighten his braces? Who else will listen to those silly sports games with him? I have to be near him. He needs me.

Your friend,

Catherine

Adventures in Jamestown
Softcover • ISBN 9780310713920

Londoner Abigail Matthews, a daring adventurer, moves to Jamestown and then Henricus, Virginia, where she comes to know Pocahontas, who was captured by the settlers. Her best friend Elizabeth Walton, still in England, encourages Abigail to see past her hurt and anger to befriend this most unlikely of companions. Excellent for educators and home-school use.

Escape on the Underground Railroad
Softcover • ISBN 9780310713913

Together, two girls living a world apart must outwit slave catchers
and assist a runaway South Carolina slave girl on her perilous trip
from Virginia to Canada on the Underground Railroad. Excellent for
educators and homeschool use.

Available now at your local bookstore!

Attack at Pearl Harbor
Softcover • ISBN 9780310713890

Determined to learn to fly, Meredith experiences consequences that will unwittingly provide her just what she needs when the Japanese bomb Pearl Harbor in 1941, and her best friend's determination to report on unfolding events puts her family right in the center of the story. Excellent for educators and homeschool use.

We want to hear from you. Please send your comments about this book to us in care of zreview@zondervan.com. Thank you.